I0817968

SEE HER SCREAM

(A Mia North FBI Suspense Thriller—Book 3)

Rylie Dark

Rylie Dark

Debut author Rylie Dark is author of the SADIE PRICE FBI SUSPENSE THRILLER series, comprising six books (and counting); the MIA NORTH FBI SUSPENSE THRILLER series, comprising six books (and counting); the CARLY SEE FBI SUSPENSE THRILLER, comprising six books (and counting); and the MORGAN STARK FBI SUSPENSE THRILLER, comprising three books (and counting).

An avid reader and lifelong fan of the mystery and thriller genres, Rylie loves to hear from you, so please feel free to visit www.ryliedark.com to learn more and stay in touch.

ISBN: 978-1-0943-9448-0

BOOKS BY RYLIE DARK

SADIE PRICE FBI SUSPENSE THRILLER
ONLY MURDER (Book #1)
ONLY RAGE (Book #2)
ONLY HIS (Book #3)
ONLY ONCE (Book #4)
ONLY SPITE (Book #5)
ONLY MADNESS (Book #6)

MIA NORTH FBI SUSPENSE THRILLER
SEE HER RUN (Book #1)
SEE HER HIDE (Book #2)
SEE HER SCREAM (Book #3)
SEE HER VANISH (Book #4)
SEE HER GONE (Book #5)
SEE HER DEAD (Book #6)

CARLY SEE FBI SUSPENSE THRILLER
NO WAY OUT (Book #1)
NO WAY BACK (Book #2)
NO WAY HOME (Book #3)
NO WAY LEFT (Book #4)
NO WAY UP (Book #5)
NO WAY TO DIE (Book #6)

MORGAN STARK FBI SUSPENSE THRILLER
TOO LATE (Book #1)
TOO CLOSE (Book #2)
TOO FAR GONE (Book #3)

CHAPTER ONE

David Hunter shifted uneasily in his desk chair.

He knew it would be easy enough to get the gun Mia North wanted, almost too easy.

But he also knew that it was absolutely going to get him in some boiling hot water if he got caught. Enough to ruin his life completely.

From the moment he'd gone into headquarters, that morning, he was on high alert. There were hundreds of unmarked guns in the depository. Any agent could go in and help himself.

But until that day, the thought had been out of the question in his mind. FBI agents were sworn to a code of ethics. And it was that code of ethics they were held to. The FBI trusted him not to screw around.

And until Mia North had escaped from prison, he'd trusted himself, too.

Mia North, his former partner, was a wanted fugitive who'd been on the run for the better part of a month. She'd been arrested for a murder that she insisted she hadn't committed. The whole country, and now the U.S. Marshals, were looking for her.

She was his friend. His confidant. And he'd already screwed her once, giving the testimony that put her in prison. And the more she kept insisting that she was innocent . . . the more he'd begun to believe she might be right. That powerful senate candidate Wilson Andrews had set her up to get her out of the way, since she'd been after his serial killer brother, Jerry. Too many strange things had happened since, and it all resulted in her communicating to him that she needed a gun if she was ever going to prove her innocence.

But the second he had the gun in his hand, something in him had shifted. Until that moment, he'd been proud of his work as a federal agent. The moment he placed the gun in his pocket, he crossed a line he'd been straddling, and was now firmly on the wrong side of the law.

Just like she was.

And with every step he took away from that storage room, he felt worse and worse. Like he was endangering everything that meant something to him. For what?

Because right is right, he told himself. *And Mia deserves this chance.*

Now, in his cubicle, he faced the imposing form of U.S. Marshal Kane Wilcox. He'd been just about to put the gun into his briefcase when the agent cornered him. Now, Wilcox sat across from him, his feet up on the desk, looking like he owned the place. And maybe he did. The jerk had been slowly weaseling his way into the Dallas Fort Worth police force, and what was even more unbelievable was that Lieutenant Briggs, who seemed to have an aversion to all Feds, had actually let him.

Hunter's pulse pounded under his collar as he closed his briefcase, still feeling the gun burning a hole in his pocket.

He gritted his teeth and leveled his gaze at the Marshal, who'd just accused him of exactly what he'd been doing—helping Mia North. "I don't know what you're getting at."

"Well, I still think back to that night. How your prime suspect was laid out for you, so nicely like that. Whoever did it might as well have left you a greeting card."

Hunter lowered his gaze to his blotter. "And?"

"And," he said, leaning forward and smirking. "I think you know who did it."

Of course, he did. It was all Mia. Mia had been in the background, laying low. But she was instrumental in finding the last killer. Without her know-how and grit, the case would've still been confusing the hell out of the Dallas Fort Worth PD. He'd kept it quiet, pretended like it was all his work. And this was the thanks he got?

He shrugged. "I think you're wrong."

"That's funny. Because I just got back from the lab and it's like I thought. Your partner's fingerprints and blood samples are all over that house. On the knife. On the floor. On the suspect. Everywhere."

He froze. They'd gotten their woman, and she'd confessed. Open and shut case. No need for lab tests. "I didn't order any—"

"Yeah. I did." His smile widened.

"Last I checked, this wasn't your case. What authorization do you have to—"

"Believe me, it's all in order."

Somehow, he'd been anticipating this. He'd seen the way the Marshal had stalked about the place. He'd watched him crouch in front of the blood, staring at it with great interest. He should've known he'd have collected those samples.

"Fine. Well," he began, ready to tell him he had no idea what it meant. "Like I said, I never—"

Wilcox slammed his fists down on the desk. "You knew Mia was there because she called you. When we were in the interrogation room with Donovan, you received a phone call. From her. Admit it."

He sucked in a breath. "I'll admit no such thing. Can you please leave my—"

"No, Hunter."

He looked up. His boss, Special Agent in Charge Pembroke of the Dallas Field Office, was standing in the doorway. He stepped in and closed the door. David Hunter's stomach dropped.

"I think this is something you need to answer for, Agent," Pembroke said, crossing his arms. "Are you helping Mia North?"

He sat there, both answers, yes and no, hovering on his lips. He could tell the truth, and get in some trouble. Maybe lose his job. Lie, and down the road, he'd end up in prison. Every option sucked. For him, and for his son, Louie.

So he said nothing.

Agent Pembroke leaned in more. "Answer, me, Agent. If there's anything you want to tell us, now is the time."

He felt a bead of sweat trickle down his ribcage. He did his best to meet his supervisor's eyes, to not flinch. Then he said, as calmly as he could, "I already told you. She called me once when she was in prison, and that's the last time I spoke to her. I have not seen or heard from Mia since her escape."

Pembroke glanced at Wilcox, who stared David Hunter down with ice-blue eyes, unblinking. The man was all hard edges and angles, and probably had never smiled a day in his fifty-some years. His expression said everything: *Bullshit.*

Hunter matched it with a shrug. "Whatever you're fishing for, Agent, I can't help you."

Pembroke nodded. "There, you see? Let's give up this charade. Hunter's never given anyone reason to doubt him. So instead of beating this dead horse, let's put some more bodies into tracking—"

Wilcox reached into his jacket and slapped something down on the desk. When he removed his hand, a deep feeling of dread engulfed David Hunter.

"You know what this is?"

Hunter rolled his eyes. "Of course I do. It's a warrant." He lifted it and read it. "To search my house."

Wilcox watched him carefully. "And?"

He shrugged and tossed it down, feigning disinterest. "And what?"

"And the Dallas Fort Worth Police are in the process of executing it right now." He leaned forward. "Does that concern you?"

"Should it?"

He already knew the answer. Yes. The moment he saw the warrant, his mind had gone cycling through every room of his house. He had the burner phone he used to communicate with her on his person, the gun in the pocket of his blazer. He destroyed everything else. He didn't think he'd left any evidence of his interactions with Mia around his house. But what if he had? They'd try to connect even the smallest thing to her, and it'd put him in the same place Mia had been, a month ago . . .

He couldn't worry about that, now. He had to stay cool.

Miraculously, Wilcox did something Hunter hadn't expected.

He broke his gaze, shook his head, and ran a hand through his scrubby military haircut. "We'll see," he growled. "And if we find so much as a post-it note, tying you to Mia, your ass is grass."

He snorted. "Well, good luck proving that in court. Because Mia and I were partners for three years. I have lots of stuff with her name on it in my house."

Wilcox gave him a hard sneer, spun, and stalked out of the office, leaving him alone with Pembroke.

Special Agent in Charge Pembroke was a good guy. A hardass, but even and fair. Pembroke might have liked Mia better than him, but he still looked after his people with the care of a mother hen.

When Wilcox was gone, he slid into the chair across from him, shaking his head and sighing loudly. Her dragged his hands down his face. "Some day, huh?"

"Tell me about it," he said, relaxing a little. "They're not going to find anything, boss."

He waved that away. "Of course they're not. But let them have their fun."

Hunter stared at him. His supervisor looked absolutely beaten, ten years older, as if this ordeal had taken a huge toll on him. Pembroke was a tiger—he liked to fight. He'd have had no problem getting the kibosh put on this, if he wanted. He'd have run it straight up the ranks, making sure everyone in charge knew it was a waste of time and resources.

So that meant only one thing.

Pembroke wasn't saying so. He'd never say so. But he believed there was a kernel of truth to their accusations.

"Look," he said in an uncharacteristically quiet voice, lacing his fingers in front of him. "I need to talk to you about something."

Hunter leaned forward. As he did, he felt the hard side of the gun in his pocket, bang against the front of the desk. Whatever his boss was about to say, he knew it was nothing good. "Yeah?"

"I spoke with the Dees today."

FBI Director John Dees, out of D.C., Pembroke's boss. The big man. In the FBI, the buck stopped with him. Hunter had never met him—he wasn't important enough to even be on his radar.

At least, he'd thought.

Now, he got the feeling he *was* on the FBI Director's radar, and not for a very good reason.

"Why?" he asked, stiffening.

"Well, David, we've agreed that it makes sense that you take a leave of absence," he said, averting his eyes. "For your protection."

He gritted his teeth. "Protection?"

"Yeah. It's going to get pretty ugly here before it gets better, so I think that it makes sense you're not anywhere near here. Obviously, it'll be paid, and only temporary," he said giving him a thumbs-up. "You're a good agent. We wouldn't want to lose you."

"And forcing me out of the office is the way to do that? What am I supposed to do about my caseload?"

"Anderson will fill in while you're out." He managed a tight smile that didn't quite reach his eyes.

"Anderson? He's a dinosaur! He doesn't even—"

"He knows enough. And he's been on the force longer than you have. Before you came on, he worked with her." He studied David for a moment and the smile widened. "Really, with all the press and shit flying around here, consider it a blessing."

A blessing? What the hell? Hadn't he proven how much he loved this job? How much he'd rather be here, than anywhere else? He hadn't worked and clawed for this position, going through rounds of applications and interviews and the academy, just to sit home on his ass all day. He'd sacrificed his marriage because of his dedication to the job. It wasn't just his livelihood. It was his *life*.

And now, he felt like he'd just been shoved out of an airplane without a parachute. This was no blessing, that was for damn sure.

"But what if I—"

"*Hunter*," he said, in a tone that made it clear this wasn't up for discussion. "You'll be expected to vacate the office immediately."

Yet another indication that this wasn't just a happy little vacation. He felt like a criminal himself as his boss knocked on his desk, stood up, and vacated his cubicle without another word.

David looked around the four gray walls of his little home away from home, and shook his head. His face steamed. He pulled on his collar. He tried to tell himself that this was a good thing, that he'd have more time with Louie, his son.

But he sure as hell didn't feel good. Because though they were framing it as a good thing, he knew the powers that be would be watching him like a hawk.

And he felt even worse when he stood up and his hand hit against the gun in his pocket.

The gun he'd stolen from his employer, to give to a wanted fugitive.

It was too late to try to put it back. And he'd promised her, because he knew she needed it. He'd have to find some way to get it into Mia North's hands.

But how could he, now?

CHAPTER TWO

Mia North sat in the parking lot of a convenience store on Seventh Street, hood pulled tight over her head, drumming her fingers on the steering wheel.

Earlier that night, she'd watched Wilson Andrews, the man due to be elected by a landslide to the state senate this November—not to mention, the man responsible for ruining her life— engaged in a shady, back-alley deal with some thug. An envelope had been exchanged.

"You understand what needs to happen?"

That's what the All-American, baby-kissing, wonder-candidate had said, right before the deal.

She wasn't sure of much, but it'd had all the markings of a hit. Was this the same guy who'd killed Ellis Horvath, the man she'd gone to prison for murdering? There were so many questions, and she'd been trying to answer them, to put the pieces of the puzzle together for so long, only to run against obstacle upon obstacle.

Case in point, tonight.

She'd gone out, expecting to tail the guy. It wasn't her first rodeo; she'd performed surveillance dozens of times before. Somehow, though, she'd lost him in downtown Dallas traffic, and only caught up with him by sheer luck when she found his car, a tan sedan, a few hours later, parked in front of the Sip n' Shake Convenience Store.

She watched the large man in the cargo jacket and skull cap emerge a few moments later, sipping on a giant-sized soft drink.

When he got out, instead of heading straight to his car, he stopped in front of the trash can. He tossed the straw wrapper inside, looked around, then reached into the pocket of his jacket, pulled something out, and dropped it in. It made a loud, clanking noise that Mia could hear, even from across the parking lot.

Now, that's very interesting, she thought, watching him get into his car and head north on Seventh.

The second he did, she pulled out of her space and up to the curb in front of the store. Making sure her hood was pulled tight around her face, she got out, threw off the lid to the can, and reached inside, rifling around. She found it, among the trash, at the very bottom of the bag.

Just as she'd thought. A gun.

Quickly pocketing it, she rushed for the car and took off, hoping she could find the hitman's car. She caught up with him a few lights down on Seventh. He had his window down and was smoking a cigarette, looking as relaxed as could be.

She followed him to a row home that wasn't too far away from the place where she'd been framed for the murder of Ellis Horvath. As she drove, thoughts of that night came back to her.

She'd acted rashly, barreling into the empty warehouse without waiting for David. But she'd had a good reason. Ellis had been stalking her daughter, Kelsey, and she'd received a call from him, luring her to the place. She wanted to confront him, once and for all.

And then she'd found him there, shot dead.

By whom, she didn't know. She hadn't seen the real culprit.

But Mia had been the perfect patsy. She had motive, opportunity, means . . .

And that bastard Wilson Andrews knew it. He'd done it to cover his own ass, ruining her life in the process.

So, for the thousandth time, the same mantra played in her head: *If it's the last thing I do, I'm going to make sure he goes down.*

She pulled to the curb down the street from where the tan sedan parked and watched as the hefty man in the skull cap got out of the car and climbed the steps to his home, then fumbled at the front stoop for the keys.

This wasn't a good neighborhood to be caught in after dark. All kinds of illegal activities were happening on these streets, which was why Mia knew it well. But those activities were the least of her problems right now.

Mia stared at him a moment, wondering. Was he the man who'd shot Horvath, that night, too? Or had that crooked cop Reynolds done it, and this guy had been hired to off Reynolds?

So intent was her gaze on him, that her fingers missed the door handle twice before she was able to pull it open. When she did, she slipped out, then moved into the shadows, hugging the building as she advanced toward his house.

She was only a house away when he finally found his key, opened the door, and went inside.

Mia stood outside, moving slowly and trying to act inconspicuous as she watched the lights in the downstairs area flip on. She glanced around, but didn't see anyone else, so she stood near the stairs, watching and waiting. It was after midnight. He'd probably go off to bed soon.

Sure enough, the downstairs lights turned off a moment later.

She hesitated for only a second, thinking of the hit this man was about to perform. She couldn't wait.

Quickly, she climbed the stairs to the front and tried the door. She easily picked the lock. She pushed it open, slowly, and peered into the darkness. The only light seemed to be coming from the upstairs hallway. She could hear water running somewhere in the house—he was probably getting ready for bed.

She slipped in and closed the door behind her, then turned on her phone flashlight and cast its beam upon a living room with a giant wall-sized television, a few gamer chairs, and nothing else.

Who is this guy? she wondered, looking around for some discarded mail or something that would answer the question. Meanwhile, upstairs, she heard the floorboards shifting, the sound of water, growing louder.

She stooped in front of a pile of old *Playboy* magazines. *People still read this?* she thought, turning it over, hoping to find an address label.

Nothing.

This man was Mr. Anonymous.

She could probably look up property records online, but there was a good chance that this guy was just renting. *Probably* even from Wilson Andrews, considering he'd bought up quite a bit of real estate in the worst neighborhoods. There were rumors he was a slumlord, charging people crazy rent for squalid little hovels. But of course, with Wilson Andrews, nothing stuck.

What I really need to do is find the guy's wallet, she thought. *And I have a pretty good idea where that is.*

She went to the foot of the stairs and looked up. It was dangerous, sure. But she'd been tailing this guy all night. It wasn't enough just to have the gun. She needed more.

She slowly started to climb the worn treads, trying to be as light on her feet as possible.

Before she could even take the third step, something reached out from behind her, placing a hand on her hood and yanking her back. She let out a surprised yelp as she stumbled backwards, her back crashing into a wall. An arm pressed up against her throat, cutting her air supply.

"What the hell are you doing in my house?"

It was the hit-man she'd been tailing. He had a round, grizzled face, an old, pink, hairless scar stretching through the dark stubble on his chin. He shoved her back roughly, his eyes narrowed slits.

"Answer me." He pushed harder, crushing her windpipe. "You've been following me, huh?"

She gritted her teeth. How could she have been so stupid? Her word was a breath: "Maybe."

"I can call the cops. They'll come and arrest your ass, you know. And I will. You got nothing on me."

"I found the gun you tried to ditch at the convenience store."

His scowl deepened. "Did you, now?"

She nodded.

His frown gave way to a smile. Then he chuckled. "I bet you did. The boss said I'd probably have a bitch tailing me. He told me to watch out for you. But why?" He moved back and looked her over. "You ain't nothin' but a little thing. What could you possibly do to me?"

As he said those words, he loosened his grip slightly, and she was able to breathe more comfortably.

Big mistake. Only, he didn't realize it yet.

Instead, he reached up and pulled a lock of her hair free of the hood, and twirled it in his other finger. "How about you give me that gun back, and I won't make this unpleasant for you. We got a deal?"

She smiled sweetly at him. Then, with one, quick movement, she raised her leg and kneed him squarely in the crotch.

He doubled forward, breathless, eyes wide in surprise. Taking advantage of the moment, she pushed off the wall and kicked him in the face. He stumbled back against the railing, his weight splintering it into pieces, wooden spindles flying everywhere. His hands fanned out for some support, but finding none, he landed with a crash in a pile of broken debris on the scuffed linoleum floor.

She jumped onto his chest and stooped over him, grabbing him by the t-shirt. She took one of the sharp splinters of wood and held it up so its point pierced his throat, showing him she meant business.

"Listen to me," she growled, fisting it in her hand and bringing her face down low so she could smell his rancid breath. "I don't want to hurt you. I just want information. What's your name and who do you work for?"

He shook his head slightly. She grabbed his t-shirt tighter and shoved him down, hard, so the back of his head slammed against the floor.

"Tell me!"

"Ernie. Um—Ernie Modesto. I don't work for—I don't—"

"Bullshit! You work for Wilson Andrews. I saw you take money from him outside the hotel. Admit it."

He nodded. "Okay, okay. I did. Just this one time."

"For what? What did he have you do?"

He swallowed. "I don't know. I had to—I had to off some corrupt cop. Said he had it coming to him. That's all."

Reynolds. He killed Reynolds. And yeah, Kevin Reynolds might have been a corrupt cop who was there when the whole thing went down, but did he deserve death? No, that was only to protect Wilson Andrews's reputation.

But that wasn't what she cared most about.

She gripped his t-shirt tighter and shook him harder. "I know Wilson Andrews had me framed because he didn't want me sticking my nose into his brother's murders. Who helped him? Was it Reynolds? The cop you killed?"

He shook his head. "I don't know! I don't know anything! I just do what the politician tells me. That's all. I—" He blinked. "Wait. Are you Mia North? The one in the news? The agent who's been running from the cops?"

She stiffened. She didn't want to be identified by anyone. Even this criminal who'd never go to the cops and report seeing her.

But she did believe him when he said that he didn't know anything. Wilson Andrews probably made sure his associates knew as little as possible.

"Listen to me, you son of a bitch," she said, pressing the sharpened weapon closer to his bobbing Adam's apple. "Tell me exactly what he said when he had you kill Reynolds."

"He told me to go to his apartment. He gave me a key he'd had made. So I just waited there until the guy came home, surprised him as he was getting in. It was easy peasy. That's all."

She winced, remembering the state of the body she'd found. "That didn't look easy. You beat him to death. You didn't shoot him."

He blinked. "You saw? How did you--"

"I saw enough."

"Yeah, well . . . I was going to shoot him, but I saw a kid across the hall when I was going in. I thought he might hear the gunshot and call the cops."

"He didn't say anything to you before you killed him?"

His eyes lit up. "As a matter of fact, he did. He begged for his life like a little sissy. Then he said something about a girl. How he should've come forward back then."

"What girl?"

Ernie shrugged. "I don't know. He kept babbling about it. How he was sorry. How he should've come forward back then, when he first found out about it. He kept saying that, over and over again, how he regretted it."

Mia straightened, thinking. That could've referred to the kidnapping of Sara Waverly. Maybe Reynolds had known about Jerry Andrews's sick obsession with young girls, too. Wilson Andrews certainly had, and he'd gone through a lot to keep it quiet, to preserve his family's name.

"What did he give you the money for, tonight?" she said softly.

"That was for the hit. He promised me half when I agreed, half when I finished."

"But I heard him say, *You understand what needs to happen?* What was he referring to?"

"He wanted me to dispose of the gun. He was kind of pissed when he found out I was still holding onto it. That's it."

She wasn't sure if she could believe him, so she stared into his eyes for a beat. She saw panic there. She slowly let him go, and stood up, backing towards the door, still holding the sharpened spindle as her weapon. He slowly rose onto his elbows and watched her.

The scumbag had killed a cop. Even if he was a dirty one, he was a murderer. But as much as she wanted to bring him in, in her current state, there was nothing she could do.

"Let's keep this little meeting between us, shall we?" she said, dropping the weapon and slipping out the door. She had to find a place to lay low tonight, but tomorrow, she'd need to get in touch with David.

CHAPTER THREE

Since Mia's escape from custody, she'd bounced around from place to place in about a 200-mile radius of Dallas, never staying in the same area more than one night. Some places had proved much better than others. The Irving Arms cottages was a perfect, remote hole-in-the-wall for lying low, which was why Mia was staying there, now, for the third time since her escape.

The old couple who ran it didn't believe in credit cards. Cash only, which was perfect for her. They didn't even want her to sign a guest book. The "cottages" were actually little tents, spread out among a few acres of grassland, near a small lake. People there liked to stay to themselves, and so the last two times she'd stayed, she'd gotten some sorely-needed shut-eye.

This time, though, she'd found herself staring at the moonlight filtering through the canvas tent flaps, above, watching it ripple in the breeze, and thinking about how much she missed her husband Aiden, and eight-year-old daughter, Kelsey.

The sad thing was, she hadn't realized how good she'd had it. How many times had she gotten up from the dinner table early, to run off on a case? Or missed one of Kelsey's school functions? The day she'd been arrested, that's what she'd done—they'd all been enjoying themselves, but she'd insisted on going to that abandoned warehouse.

Why had she done that? If she hadn't, she'd still be home, with them. Kelsey would have a mom.

When she finally did fall asleep, she dreamed that she was in her house again, and that it was just a regular Sunday barbecue at their home in University Park. She longed for those days, days when she had nothing to worry about but making sure they had enough tequila and limes for the margaritas. She and her parents and sister Francie would sit around, talking shop, and Aiden would work the grill. They'd laugh and laugh.

She smiled as they sat on the back patio in the warm sunshine, watching Kelsey, playing basketball with her dad.

Suddenly, the doors to the house burst open, and FBI agents in full tactical gear appeared, guns drawn.

"FBI!" the shouted, "Get down on the ground!"

They threw her down onto the ground, twisting her arms behind her and throwing her into handcuffs. Somewhere, she could hear Kelsey crying. Aiden said, "Why, Mia? Why did you do it? Why did you leave us?"

She looked up to see them all staring at her, crying, as the agents yanked her up and pulled her through the house. She tried to reach for them, to call for them, but all she could do was watch, mute, as the agents carried her farther and farther away.

"No!" she finally screamed, muscling her way free.

Before she could, fully escape them, though, her house burst into flames. There, among the ashes, she saw a burned body. It wasn't Kelsey, or Aidan . . .

It was a woman, made entirely of flames, from her long hair to her toes. Her hands were stretched out, her eyes black pinpoints, her mouth opened wide to an impossibly black hole. Her voice said, "Please . . . help me . . ." and her hands reached out and grabbed ahold of her shoulders . . .

But then Mia's eyes opened, and she found herself sitting upright in the cot, the morning sunshine spreading across the wood-planked floor of the cottage-tent. Her skin was coated in a cold sweat.

She stretched her arms up over her head, feeling sore, and yawned. Well, at least she'd gotten some sleep.

She pulled the sheet off her body and swung her legs off the side of the cot. As she did, she heard the sound of something buzzing faintly. At first, she thought it was just the rustle of leaves overhead, but then she realized it was coming from underneath her pillow.

Her phone!

David.

Of course it was him. She'd texted him last night to tell him not to worry about the gun, after all. She reached for the phone, ready to answer the call, when she noticed the number was an unfamiliar one. That was odd. He was the only one who had that number. But David had lost his burner before; maybe he'd gotten another.

Or maybe it was someone else.

At first, she thought that she'd let it ring to voicemail. She did, but it started to ring again. Same number.

Eventually, curiosity got the better of her. She pressed the button to accept the call and brought the phone to her ear, uttering a simple, "Yes."

"Mia."

Her stomach dropped. That wasn't David's voice. Not even close. He had an unmistakably low timber to his voice. This male speaker's voice was decidedly higher-pitched. Familiar, and yet . . . she couldn't place it.

"Who is this?"

There was a slight chuckle. "I'm surprised you even have to ask that, after all we've been through, North."

It hit her right away. Marcus Shields. FBI tech guy extraordinaire. In her head, she saw him, the skeleton-skinny guy with the too-long black curls, who wore an AC/DC t-shirt every chance he got. They'd gone through the academy together, though he'd always had that computer-geek vibe, as opposed to her background in law enforcement and criminal justice. He'd helped her on a number of cases over the years, providing tech support. She wouldn't consider him a good friend, but he *was* a friend. Still, she was cautious.

"How did you get this number?"

More laughter. "Like you even have to ask? You remember what I do for a living? I know it's been a while since we worked on a case together, but give me more credit than that."

"Hmm . . ." she said, not sure where he was going with that. Did that mean he was going to turn her in?

"Here's the deal. Hunter's being investigated for a possible connection to you. And they put me on the case."

Panic flooded her. "So?"

"Anyway, I was able to use video surveillance of the times David was on the phone, ping the local cell tower, and trace it to this number. Voila." A pause. "How are the Irving Arms Cottages this time of year?"

She cringed. *Oh, no.* She was busted. *They* were busted.

"I don't know what you're talking about," she said, wishing she'd never answered the phone. The last thing she wanted was to get him in hot water. David Hunter would help her, because he was just a good guy and couldn't say no to a friend in need. But he had sole custody of his son, Louie. If he got sent away, it'd ruin the poor kid's life.

"Sorry, Mia, but this kind of proof is air-tight. You can't bluff your way out of it."

She swallowed. "You told Pembroke, then."

To her surprise, he said, "Actually, no."

She stood up and began to pace across the tent in her bare feet. This was bad. She hadn't figured Marcus Shields for a snake, but everyone had their price. Maybe he saw a way of benefiting from this situation, and was weaseling her into blackmail.

"What do you want from me?" She bit out every word with effort.

"Hey, listen," he said, sounding embarrassed. "It's nothing like that. Nothing at all. I just . . . Mia, you and I worked together a long time. And I think we grew to respect each other. And this stuff they're saying you did? I don't believe any of it. A lot of us don't. We're all pulling for you."

She frowned. If he'd made it a point to get her number, just so he could give her that pep talk . . . she didn't believe it. There was something else. "And?"

"And, like I said, I respect you . . ."

Why did it sound like he was stalling? Was he trying to keep her there, in one place, for some reason?

She hurried to the front of the tent, lifted the flap, and looked out, half-expecting to see the entire Dallas Police, streaming into the parking lot at the front of the facility. But it was quiet as ever, a nice warm day with no clouds on the horizon as all.

"Marcus. I'm sure you didn't call me to tell me what a great job I'm doing," she said, going back in and pulling out a change of clothes from her backpack. He was making her antsy, and that meant she had to move. "So give it to me straight. Did you tell anyone where I am?"

"No! I'm serious. I promise, Mia. But look, all right? There's a case, and the second I heard about it, I thought about you."

She'd been trying to wiggle out of her shirt without dropping her phone, but now she paused. She lowered the phone and put it on speaker. "Why's that?"

"Because I thought you'd find it interesting. Remember the Carrie Winters case?"

She froze. How could she forget? It was one from the beginning of her career in the FBI. The poor girl, barely eighteen, found in the middle of the desert, burned to a skeleton. She'd been doused in gasoline and left there to die.

Try as she had, it had haunted her for years afterwards . . . because though Mia was known for digging up evidence on cold cases, that one? It had never been solved.

A feeling of déjà vu gripped her, as she remembered her dream. The flaming girl, reaching out to her. An odd coincidence, nothing more. Or was it?

"Yeah, down near the border, right? Del Rio? What about it?"

"Well, there's been two more girls who have disappeared recently. They've gone missing for months, so their families think they've run away. Only for them to be found, a few months later, burned, in the desert. Just like Carrie."

Still half-dressed, she fell to her bed with a thud. "No kidding. It's been so long since--"

"Eight years. Yeah."

"Who's investigating it?"

"Couple guys on the force looked into the first one, but got nowhere. I think they were down in Del Rio a total of five minutes before determining they didn't have enough evidence. The second one? Well—" He paused, and for a second she thought she heard his voice crack. "It just happened. I mean, they just found her body yesterday."

Something occurred to her. Marcus played assist on a lot of cases, but he didn't work on his own. "Okay, Marcus . . . but why are you calling me about it?"

"Because of your connection with the last one. You're the best at these things, and I was thinking you'd want to know . . ."

"I didn't solve that last one, if you'll remember."

"I know. But you care. You don't see the victims as just a number, like some of the guys around here." He inhaled sharply, then let it out. "And . . . Rachel—she's the girl who they just found—she's my niece."

She let out the breath she'd been holding. Oh. Now it made sense. Now, she wasn't concerned about the police showing up in front of her tent. This was personal for him. "I'm so sorry, Marcus."

"Yeah, well . . .," he trailed off for a moment, and when he spoke again, his voice was deeper. "It's been a shock. Rachel didn't always get along with her parents, so they thought she'd run away. This really leveled them. So I promised my sister I'd do everything I can for her. And that meant calling you."

"I understand. But here's what you need to do. You have to let the other guys handle it. It only just happened. Give them some time to—"

"You know time is of the essence. And you know they're going to run in circles around the government bureaucracy while this bastard gets away."

She did know that. These past few weeks of operating above the law had taught her that a good number of cases could've been solved easily had they not had to follow official FBI procedure. That's why she'd been successful so far. She'd had close scrapes, but she'd been lucky. It was only a matter of time before that luck ran out.

She let out a short laugh. "Marcus. I'm not actually in the place right now to help anyone but myself."

"You helped David solve that last case."

"Yes, but—"

"And face it. You can do a lot more than we can, under the radar."

She sighed. "But how long will I stay under the radar, if I keep dancing so close to crime scenes, Marcus? I can't. It's too dangerous."

"Yeah. But it'll be even more dangerous for you if I call Pembroke and tell him what I know about you."

She closed her eyes and gripped the phone tightly. There it was. The rub. Just what she needed—another person who knew her secret and could blab at any moment to the authorities. "So you are blackmailing me?"

"Listen, Mia. I don't want to. I swear, it's the last thing I want to do. But I need your help."

"You do know that I'm a little wrapped up in other things, right?"

"Yeah . . . obviously. But could you? Just look into it a little? See what you might find?"

She was already shaking her head. The whole conversation, the thought of her cover being blown, was too much for her. She grabbed her things, took a last look around the tent to make sure she hadn't left anything behind, and stepped out into the warm sunlight. "I've got to go. Can you give me a little time to think about it?"

His lips twitched. "I don't—time is of the essence—"

"And I don't see you have much of a choice."

"Fine. But only until tonight. Let me give you a secure number you can reach me on."

He rattled it off, and she committed it to memory, intending to type it into her contacts the second she got off. "Got it."

"Thanks, Mia. And stay safe."

She ended the call, plugged the number into her contacts, and stepped up the path toward the main office of the cottage rental. She needed to get a move on if she was going to check out that detail Ernie had provided, about that girl Reynolds had spoken about before he was killed.

Climbing into the front seat of her beater car, she shook her head. *Stay safe*. Ironic, considering he wanted her to jump right into the fire again, where nothing would be safe at all.

CHAPTER FOUR

You'd have to be a complete idiot to think that's a good idea.

Those were the words that cycled through Mia's head as she drove toward Dallas. In her head, they were spoken in David's voice, because he'd always been the cautious one. The voice of reason.

Even that tragic night of Ellis Horvath's murder, had he been there, he'd have told her that. And maybe all of this could've been prevented.

Which was why, as curious as she was about the case of the burned girls, she couldn't commit. David had thought it foolish, looking into Jerry Andrews. Though he'd given her the details on the case of the murdered college co-ed, more recently, he'd quickly tried to reel her in, so she wouldn't get caught.

Yes. He'd definitely think she was a total idiot for looking into this case.

Besides, she had her own problems to deal with.

Stop worrying about Marcus. Concentrate.

The previous night, before she'd fallen asleep, she'd thought more about what Ernie had said. Kevin Reynolds had mentioned a girl. She was someone he wished he'd have come forward about. At first, Mia had thought that might be Sara Waverly, one of Jerry Andrews's first victims. But the more she thought about it, the more that didn't seem right. Sara had been found alive, so why have regrets?

No . . . it felt like he was referring to something else. Something far worse.

As she drove, she grabbed her phone and pulled up the article she'd read from a few days before: *Wilson Andrews Gearing up for campaign event in University Park.*

The event was due to be held at the Hyatt she'd visited the night before, where she'd seen him make that shady deal. As far as Mia was concerned, he was the logical connection to whoever this girl was. After all, it was well-known that he had mistresses. Maybe one of them had been underage, or had been hurt or killed during an encounter with the politician, and Reynolds had been instructed to cover it up.

She drove into the parking lot of the Hyatt, keeping a low profile, with her hood up and her sunglasses on. It was still early, but the place was bustling with people, going in and out of the double doors of the conference room attached to the hotel. No doubt, the most prominent Dallas society would be there, all of Andrews's top donors.

Her stomach roiled, uneasy. It was absolutely sick how some people were so untouchable. Andrews had committed a lot of vile, illegal acts in order to protect his serial killer brother, and he'd still come out of it smelling like a rose.

As she stared at the doors of the conference room, she clenched her fists. If only she could figure out what Reynolds had been talking about.

What girl?

She grabbed her phone and googled *Dallas Missing Teen.*

The results that came back—mostly articles from *The Dallas Morning News,* were spotty. Some were from years ago. Some were males. In some, the teenager had been found. It wasn't the kind of comprehensive crime data she could get if she'd typed her search criteria into the FBI files.

If she was still an FBI agent, it'd be so easy. She'd just ask Marcus to run a list of area teenagers who'd disappeared or been murdered in the last year, and have the data in minutes. That could get her somewhere.

Mia kept scrolling, and as if on cue, an article about Carrie Winters appeared. Carrie Winters, or the original girl who'd been found murdered, eight years ago.

Maybe she could get Marcus to help her. It would be easy . . . *if* she agreed to scratch his back, first.

Still unsure, she sunk down into her spot in the parking lot, watching the commotion of the event that would be happening later that night, and feeling powerless.

Whenever she felt that way, her thoughts always turned to Aiden and Kelsey.

They lived in University Park, just a few miles away from that very spot. Probably, at this time of morning, they were just getting ready to head off—Kelsey to elementary school, and Aiden to his job as an IT manager.

Her heart ached at the thought of the role she used to play in their busy mornings—making sure everyone was up, putting together brown-bag lunches, wiping the chocolate milk moustache from Kelsey's face before packing her backpack and shuttling her off to her bus stop on the corner in the family SUV. Back then, she'd considered so much of it to be a chore, but now, she longed for it.

She longed to stroke Kelsey's soft hair and kiss her on the head, smelling her shampoo. It had been so long. The arrest had happened months ago. Soon, Kelsey would be a different girl, someone who didn't remember those little love notes she used to pack sometimes, into her lunches.

Almost without realizing it, she was already turning the wheel and heading toward University Park. The tree-lined neighborhood was the perfect place for raising kids. When she and Aiden had picked it out, she'd been eight months pregnant with Kelsey, and there had been so many kids running around the neighborhood. She'd been sold when she saw the tiny baseball field at the end of the road, and all the kids, playing in one of the cul de sacs.

Now, there were a bunch of kids, all running for the corner. When she pulled around the corner and looked in her rear-view mirror, she realized why. A bus was lumbering up behind her.

She checked the faces of the kids, looking for Kelsey. All she wanted to do was see her. Just once.

But the kids climbing onto the bus were older. It was probably for the junior high.

When the bus pulled away, she drove a little more, down the street, until her home came into view. Their SUV was still parked in the driveway, which meant that they hadn't left for the day.

Tears pricked at the corners of her eyes. The loneliness had never felt so heavy.

She took a deep breath and let it out, shakily, waiting for the door to open and for the loves of her life to appear. She squeezed the steering wheel in her hands, the temptation thick to get out and run to her home. It felt so natural to just go in there, say, "I'm home!" and hug her family. Only for a moment. A minute, that's all she'd need to satisfy the need inside her for the time being.

She could.

And yet, if she did, she knew it'd be worse for all of them.

It was bad for her to even be here. The FBI had been surveilling the house, expecting she might try to make contact. She knew what that entailed—bugs, drones, hidden cameras. She knew that just because there wasn't a police car parked outside, didn't mean there weren't eyes on the place.

What if they still were there?

The skin of her neck prickled, and she suddenly felt, very strongly, like she was being watched. She glanced down the road in the rear-view mirror, to see if anyone was following her. Then she looked back toward the two massive maple trees in the front of the house, and she thought she saw something there, among the leaves.

A camera? A drone.

She squinted, and she saw it move, a lens catching the sunlight and glinting for a split second.

They were watching her.

Quickly, her heart beating hard and aching even harder, she shifted into drive and took off.

The moment she stopped at the red light of the intersection outside the development, surrounded by a number of other cars, she heard them.

Police sirens, coming closer. She saw the lights, down on the main road, and stiffened, silently looking up at the light, begging it to turn green.

It didn't. She glanced at the light on the main drag, willing it to turn yellow. But it stayed solidly green.

Shit, she thought to herself, glancing in her rear-view mirror. But there was another car there. She was boxed in.

Trapped.

The moment the police car reached the corner, the light turned green. She was close enough to see the officer, and though she blinked away quickly, there was a brief moment of eye contact. She tried to keep calm and follow the flow of traffic, hoping he wouldn't notice as she made the left turn onto the two-lane highway.

She navigated around the other cars and punched on the gas, trying to go as fast as possible without drawing attention to herself.

But just at the moment she thought she'd escaped, she saw the red and blue flashing lights in her rear-view mirror, bearing down upon her.

CHAPTER FIVE

"Perfect," Mia said aloud, swerving around a car and into the fast lane. Sirens blaring, the police car behind her was slowly closing the gap between them. Luckily, though, some obstinate drivers in the fast lane were not moving over to let the cops pass. She'd never been so glad to see idiot drivers on the road.

She watched as the cop car moved into the other lane, to pass on the right. It was still several car lengths away.

Up ahead, a light turned amber. She pressed on the gas and surged forward, sailing through the second it turned red. The other cars were sandwiching the cop car in. She watched in her side-view mirror as he blared on his horn, then started to pull onto the shoulder to resume the chase.

She floored it, taking off until she reached the next light, then hung a right by a Piggly Wiggly and fell in with a number of other cars. When she was in the parking lot, she turned into the service entrance and slowly drove into the back of the supermarket, where she parked between two trucks, delivering their cargo.

From there, she could see the road. When the police car sailed by, lights flashing.

She started to sigh with relief when suddenly, there was a knock on her window.

Nearly jumping to the roof of the car, she looked up to see a man in a tight, sleeveless t-shirt and backwards baseball cap, sucking on a toothpick. He motioned to her with the universal symbol to roll down her window.

She powered it down and he laughed. "Sorry if I scared you, darlin', but I think you made a wrong turn. The store's entrance is on the other side."

She let out the rest of that breath she'd been holding. "Sorry, I'm --"

"The manager of this place ain't gonna be happy to see you here. Trucks only." He pointed to a sign that said, *PARKING FOR DELIVERY VEHICLES ONLY.*

She nodded. "I'll move . . .," she began, getting ready to back out.

But something held her back. She didn't want to get out of the hiding spot. She couldn't be seen in this car again. She glanced at the trucks around her. The green one to the right of her said it was from Abilene, Texas, which was southwest of town.

That was exactly what she needed—to get out of Dodge for a while and lie low.

"Something wrong?" the man asked, still gnawing.

"Yeah . . . actually. I'm wondering . . . is that your truck?"

He looked back at her and nodded. "Pretty one, huh? I'm headed back to my wife and kids after this."

It didn't take long for her to make up her mind. She gave him her nicest smile. "I'm headed that way myself, but my car's on its last legs. You wouldn't think of giving me a ride?"

He raised an eyebrow. "You, darlin'? Sure. I'd like the company. Gets awful lonely on these roads. Where you coming from?"

"Oh, uh . . . Corpus Christi?" she said, throwing her car into reverse. "And I'm visiting my boyfriend in Abilene, so this is great. It's a real blessing my car started making noise when it did."

She moved the car out and parked it near the dumpsters, then grabbed her bag and found him giving her a questioning look. "What about your car?"

"Oh, I'll come back and get it later," she said with a wave. She grabbed the handle and hoisted herself up, then opened the door to find a neat cab. It smelled slightly like cigarettes, but mostly like the pine air freshener, dangling from the window. When he was settled beside her, she said, "Thank you, this is great."

He extended a hand. "I'm Cal. And you are . . .?"

"Susan," she lied.

"All right, Susan. Nice to meet you. Where you headed in Abilene?"

"Uh . . . you don't have to take me the whole way. Really, as far as you can take me would be perfect."

"You got it," he said, starting the engine and pulling out. "So, you live in Corpus Christi and your boyfriend's in Abilene, eh? Long distance relationship?"

She nodded.

"What's keeping you separate?"

“Jobs. You know, typical sob story,” she said with a smile. “We’re both from Corpus but he got a great job . . .”

“An offer he couldn’t refuse. I get it,” he said, shaking his head. “Happened to us, too, before we got married. My wife got a teaching job in Arkansas. She almost took it.”

“What happened?”

“I proposed.” He grinned from ear to ear. “So we settled in Abilene. Can’t wait to get back to my girls. My wife and my daughters.”

Right then, she noticed a couple of crudely drawn pieces of art, on the dashboard. One of a horse, one of a family. Underneath, in red crayon, it said, *I love you, Daddy!* “You have two girls?”

“Three. Twins who are two and an older one who’s eight. I been missing their hugs.” He laughed.

Mia’s heart twisted. “I bet.”

“You have kids?”

She’d begun thinking of how Kelsey always used to draw her pictures, so many that while she hated throwing them away, there simply wasn’t enough room for them. Kelsey had written, *I love you Mommy,* a million times, tirelessly. Mia had said it to her, almost as much. And yet she’d taken those words for granted.

She’d taken all of it for granted.

“Yeah,” she said, barely a whisper. “A daughter. She’s nine.”

“She with your boyfriend?”

She shook her head, but couldn’t bring herself to say more. After a moment or two of silence, he finally got the picture that she wasn’t willing to answer. A moment after that, she took out her phone and started to scroll through it, and thankfully, he left her alone. It was exhausting, coming up with lies to satisfy his questions without giving too much of herself away.

Speaking of giving herself away, she had a decision to make, with Marcus. If she didn’t call him soon, he might spill what he knew about her, and get David in trouble. He was a straight-shooter, so she didn’t believe he’d go through with those threats, but there was always a chance that he’d be so overcome with guilt.

And she couldn’t blame him for pulling out the blackmail card. His family was in turmoil. His poor niece.

Almost as if the universe was trying to tell her something, a sign appeared on the side of the road:

Abilene 180 mi

Del Rio 420 mi

Del Rio. That godforsaken town on the U.S./Mexican border, surrounded by ranchland, mesquite trees, and thorny scrub brush. It was on the Rio Grande, and might have been a nice place to visit, had it not been the scene of such a grisly discovery. The Phantom Bridge, or *El Puente Fantasma,* as the Hispanic locals called it, just outside of town, was cursed, many of the residents had said. Because the river was deep and deceptively calm there, it had been the cause of many deaths of immigrants over the years.

But that was not how Carrie Winters had died. She'd been cursed in a different way.

Mia opened the web browser and typed in *Murder female burned Del Rio.*

The first article that came up was from yesterday:

Remains of Missing Teenager Found Near Phantom Bridge.

That was it. She remembered the name of the place. Remembered walking around the ruins there—a number of old buildings in the desert. Only the charred bones of the girl had been found, as if someone had piled what was left of her out there and started a bonfire. She read on:

Police have identified the remains found on the ground of Phantom Bridge as those of Rachel Loring, the 18-year-old Waco girl who had been missing since January.

Her charred bones were found by tourists in a field about one-hundred yards from the fort. Texas State Police said that due to the condition of the remains, homicide is suspected. No suspects have been named at this time.

Loring was last seen leaving her job at the Waco Wal-Mart on Friday, January 12th. Her parents reported her missing two hours after she was expected to return home. A police search uncovered few clues. At the time, it was believed by friends and family that she might have run away. Her mother, Emily Loring, said, "We don't know who would want to hurt our beautiful girl. A part of my heart is gone forever."

This grisly discovery is not the first to be made on the property. In January, the body of Madison Lane of Del Rio was found, and eight years ago, the body of Carrie Winters was found, both in a similar charred state on the vast 4,000 acre-property, 100 miles northwest of Del Rio, TX, near the Mexican border.

Mia looked up, the memories of the old Winters case flooding back to her. It was a horrifically sad one, made even worse because she'd never been able to find the killer. The parents in that case had also originally thought that Carrie had tried to run away, too, since she'd tried to do so before. But after the body had been found, Mia had been called in. There'd been a couple leads, and though she'd followed them doggedly, as always, they'd petered out. Eventually, she'd had to move on.

But she never forgot cases like that one. Was it a copycat? Or the same killer, gone dormant for eight years?

She scrolled down and found a school photograph of the girl, Rachel Loring. Marcus's niece. She was pretty—with long, shiny platinum hair, parted down the middle. Despite her light hair, her face was tan, and her eyes were a dark brown—just like Marcus's. She had a bit of acne on her cheeks, but it didn't subtract from her beauty. She was carrying a flag on her shoulder, part of Waco High School's band front.

Mia stared at the photograph of the girl, wondering what could've happened to her in the five months since she'd disappeared. Was she kept prisoner? Or had she simply run away, living on the streets until she met that fate?

There were too many questions, and now, Mia felt a desire growing in her to uncover the answers.

She quickly typed in the name: *Carrie Winters.*

The girl's picture popped up on her screen. It was a face that had haunted Mia for a long time. The teen's face was a little fuller, a little paler, but she was strikingly similar to Rachel Loring.

And if memory served her correctly, the other victim had been much the same. She squeezed her eyes closed and remembered something Marcus had said about a third girl. She searched for Madison Lane, from Del Rio, Texas, whose body was found a month ago, in the Phantom Bridge area.

She scrolled to her picture—another blonde, with a spray of freckles over her pert nose.

And each one of the girls was eighteen.

They had all the markings of serial killings . . . but eight years?

She had to know.

"Susan? Hey, Susan?"

She blinked and realized that Cal, next to her, was staring at her with concern. *Why is he calling me Susan? Oh, right.* "Yes?"

He pointed out the door. They were stopped at a service station with a DQ. "I was just gonna get me a Blizzard. Want anything?"

She nodded. She hadn't eaten all day. Her stomach had probably been growling loudly, while they were driving, and she'd been so deep in thought, she hadn't noticed. She reached into her pocket for her change purse. "Can you get me a sleeve of fries and a root beer?"

He waved away her five-dollar bill. "You got it, darlin'. But it's on me."

She smiled as he slammed the door and sauntered away. After all this nasty business, it was nice to know there were some good people in the world.

Mia lowered her gaze to the photograph of Madison Lane. These poor girls hadn't met one of them. That was for sure.

And even if she wasn't FBI anymore, she still felt like it was her responsibility to act, to keep the bad ones off the street. Plus, she had a feeling having Marcus Shields on her side would be very valuable for her, personally.

Letting out a sigh, she opened up a message to the number Marcus gave her, her fingers moving furiously over the keypad.

CHAPTER SIX

Marcus Shields sat in his tiny cubicle in the basement of the Dallas Field Office, staring at a blank computer screen.

Things over the past few days had been rough.

He couldn't believe his niece—the little girl he used to bounce with on the trampoline outside their house-- was gone. Dead. Murdered like some kind of animal. By some kind of animal, likely. What had gone wrong?

Sure, she'd grown up, from that cute, toothless little pigtailed angel who'd called him Mar-Mar, to a headstrong teenager. She'd gotten into her share of trouble, with drugs and parties and boys, but what teen hadn't? He'd really thought that when she disappeared, that day in January, that it was only a matter of time before they all saw her again—a little bruised, maybe, but wiser. She'd have her head on straight, and never run away from home again.

The last thing he'd expected was that call from Heather.

His older sister—she was five years his senior— had always been the strong one, the one who showed little emotion. But that call had shaken his world. She was crying so hard, she couldn't get the words out. She told him she didn't want to live anymore, with Rachel gone.

He hadn't slept at all, last night. At thirty-five, single, childless, he'd resigned himself to being a perpetual bachelor. So Heather's kids were the closest he'd ever come. Rachel and Sean. He doted on them. He sent them gifts, on their birthdays and at Christmas. He'd even set aside money for their 529s.

Rachel. Eighteen, smart, beautiful, full of dreams for the future . . . dead.

It was hard to believe, even now that he'd given it time to sink in. It all seemed like some terrible nightmare. How could it have happened? When he helped investigate these crimes, the last thing he'd ever thought was that someone in his family would be taken by one of them.

All this time, they'd thought she'd run away. She was a bit of a handful, a little resentful of her parents' constant rules and demands. She'd told them before that she was going to leave, and never come back. But she must've been kidnapped. And for five months . . . what happened? It didn't make sense. None of it did.

All he could think was that they'd wasted five months, hoping she'd learn some sense and come back on her own, when he could've been searching. Really searching. Using all the tools at his disposal to find out where she was. Whoever had her must've kept her—for five months. It was mind-boggling.

And he felt powerless. Here he was, part of the most competent criminal investigative operation on the planet, and there was little he could do.

But Mia? She was a different story. She had a way of finding things out. Digging. Scratching away until something bled and the truth came out.

He grabbed his phone and checked it for the fifteenth time that hour. No message from Mia. But there were plenty from his sister, his parents. The last one was from his mother: *I can't stop thinking of our poor baby.*

Same. He wasn't sure he'd ever sleep again, until he found out what the hell had happened.

He shoved his phone back, determined to get some work done on this case. It was some fraud thing where a woman was passing fake checks. He had to go through thousands of bank entries to see if he could find any that matched. Bullshit busywork, stuff that made his head spin.

He got about three lines down before his thoughts went to Rachel again.

This was impossible.

He banged his hand on the keyboard and the screen went black. That was one thing—as much as he loved computers, they didn't seem to return the favor. He'd accidentally turned it off.

"Shit!" he shouted, winding up to punch the thing. But then he saw the broad-bodied reflection, in the screen.

He turned, fist still raised.

Even worse. It was U.S. Marshal Kane Wilcox.

The big bear of a guy was a constant presence around the field office lately, stalking about like he owned the place, like he was better than the rest of them. Even worse, Special Agent in Charge Pembroke was just letting him. He'd taken up in Pembroke's office, and was constantly skulking around, asking questions, making every agent in the office uncomfortable.

Marcus lowered his fist and inhaled sharply. The guy smelled like a greasy-spoon diner, like bacon grease, mixed with cigarettes and old coffee. He reached over to the side of his terminal and turned the computer back on. "Yeah?"

"Shields?" Wilcox asked, not waiting for an invitation before he stepped in and lifted one ass-cheek onto his desk. He started to pull his credentials from the inside of his blazer. "I'm Special Agent—"

"I know who you are, Agent."

He stopped and tucked the credentials away. "All right. I hear you're the tech guy around here. Mind if I ask you some questions?"

He spun slightly in his task chair. "About Mia?"

Wilcox nodded. "I hear that you went to the academy with her. True?"

"Yep. I've worked with her for going on a decade." He glanced at his phone again. Ordinarily, this would be a really bad time for her to text him back, but he'd encrypted any messages that might come from the number he provided, as an extra layer of security, so he wasn't too worried. "And you won't find a better agent. She's dedicated."

"She's a convicted murderer."

"She might've been convicted, but I don't think she's a murderer," he said, matter-of-factly. "I don't care what the evidence showed. I think there was a mistake."

"Nevertheless, it's my job to—"

"I get it, I get it," he said, holding out his hands. "But it's not that I won't say anything bad about her. I just can't—because in all those years, I never saw a single thing that would make me think she could murder that dude. Not a single thing."

"Some people say she was being protective after the threats made against her daughter, and she took it too far."

He shook his head. "Like I said, I don't believe it."

Wilcox sighed and looked around. "All right. I didn't want to talk to you to get a report card on Mia North. I want to know if there's been any suspicious communication from her partner David Hunter. Anything at all that might lead you to believe she's been in contact with him."

"No."

"No?"

"I don't know how I can be clearer," he said leaning back in his chair. "I haven't seen anything suspicious at all from him. I've been monitoring all her old channels, too. There's nothing. It's clean."

Wilcox slipped off his desk and gave him a doubtful look. "I can't believe there's absolutely nothing. You've been tracking his phone calls? His texts? His—"

"Everything. Everything going in and out of his phone, I see."

"What if he had another phone?"

Shields shook his head. "If he did, he's using it apart from his regular phone. I can ping the cell tower so I know his location at all times. And I know when he's using any technology, whether or not it's registered to the FBI."

"And?"

He shrugged. "Like I said, it's clean. He's using his laptop. His phone. That's about it."

The Marshal crossed his arms over his thick chest. "Show me."

Until that moment, Marcus had had it under control. He'd known Wilcox would come and question him eventually, so he'd been preparing his answers. Practicing just how he'd handle all the curve balls the bastard wanted to throw at him. But that one threw him.

His palms instantly went slick with sweat. "Huh?"

"You heard me." He leaned forward and pointed at the computer. "Show me what you got. All the data. I want to see what he's been up to."

"I . . . I don't have it right here. It'd take me a while to assemble, and—"

He hoisted his one ass-cheek up onto the desk again, getting comfortable. "That's okay. I'll wait." He tapped his fingers on the desk and pointed to the computer. "Go on."

Marcus stared, his throat tightening until the collar of his shirt felt too tight.

Somehow, he forced out a *oh, you silly non-tech person* chuckle. Easy to do, because he'd done it enough. It was a tactic all of his fellow IT people had used, at least once in their careers—use enough technical jargon and point out enough zeros and ones, and you'd make any technophobe's eyes glaze over. Eventually, they'd often regret even asking the question. "You're welcome to, but it'll take a few hours."

He frowned. "A few hours?"

"Yeah. You know how everything in the government works. Hurry up and wait. Spend the motherlode and get shit in return. It's a lot of data so I can't keep it on the mainframe." He let out a sigh, and spread his hands wide, as if to say, *What can you do?* "Computer's been freezing up all day. That's why I was so pissed off when you came in. I'll have to input the criteria again and then it'll have to compile, so it takes—"

"Just send it to me when you have it. You have any data at all from Hunter's tech that I can look at?"

Or maybe you'll just forget you asked for it. He nodded. "Cell phone records. Those were the most pressing at the time, so I printed those out."

"Where are those?"

Marcus stood up and went to sort through the pile of papers on his desk, looking for the David Hunter folder. It was easy to find—the thickest one, right on top. As he scooped it up, the phone next to his computer lit up with a text.

Caroline: Okay.

Caroline. As in Caroline Winters, the first girl who'd been murdered by that bastard who liked to burn his victims' bodies in the desert. It was the code name he'd given to Mia, just for this purpose, so he could receive calls and texts from her without arousing suspicion.

And it was a good thing he had, because the second he glanced back, he noticed Agent Wilcox, eyeing the phone, too.

She's going for it. Hell, yes.

He had to keep his urge to do a fist-pump to himself, though. Nonchalantly, he pulled out the massive printout of David Hunter's cell phone records and dropped it into Kane Wilcox's eager hands. A nice little exercise to keep the man busy—but that was all it was. It was all squeaky clean, because the burner calls weren't part of it. Marcus had kept those at home, in a secret location. "This is it."

Wilcox took it and looked it over, running a finger down the list of numbers, losing interest after the first page. "What's this number he's calling all the time—the one with the 246 in it . . . ?"

"I believe that's his son's cell phone," Marcus said, not looking away from his computer. "And before you go asking, the other number he calls a lot is his ex-wife. A lot of coordinating goes on with child-care duties."

Wilcox grunted. From that grunt, Marcus surmised the agent hadn't gotten what he was looking for.

And he wouldn't. Not from Marcus, anyway.

Too bad. So sad.

Muttering something under his breath, the marshal slipped off the desk, still paging through the print-out, and headed for the cubicle opening. "Don't leave for the day without checking in with me," he barked over his shoulder. "I might have more questions."

"Yes, sir," Marcus muttered under his breath. Then he picked up the phone and looked at the message from Mia. It was just that one word: *Okay.*

But it was enough. Enough to get his spirits up.

Now, we're talking. Now, some things will finally start to happen.

CHAPTER SEVEN

"Beth? Beth?"

Mia was awoken by a gentle nudge to her arm. She'd been dreaming, again, about being with her family, enjoying one of those backyard barbecues, so when she cracked an eye open and saw the vast, arid Chihuahuan desert, stretching out before her, she almost wished she could go back to sleep.

She found the face of the kind old trucker from Santa Fe, staring down at her. He smiled. "Wow, you were out like a light. I was almost afraid to wake you. But it's the end of the line."

She straightened, rubbing away the crick in her neck, and swallowed, finding her throat almost as dry as her surroundings. "Where are we?"

"Bracketville. About as far as I can take you."

"Del Rio?"

He motioned down the road. "About fifteen minutes down that way."

"Thanks," she said, yawning and looking up at the sign for the Border Crossing Travel Mart. She'd have to get something to drink there. But this was perfect. It was just where she needed to be. She gathered her things and pushed open the door. "I appreciate the lift."

He gave her a salute. "Happy travels, Beth. Hope you find what you're looking for."

I hope so, too. Though she had no idea what she'd told the man. She couldn't even remember his name. Over the past few hours, she'd ridden with countless truckers, shifting her name and story every time, just in case that guy from the U.S. Marshals was still on her tail. She couldn't remember this old trucker's name, or what she'd told him she was looking for, so she simply gave him a little wave and slammed the truck door.

Then she headed into the rest stop to get that drink.

Before she could open the door, though, something captured her attention. It was a photograph of the second girl, Madison Lane, surrounded by wilting flowers and sun-battered stuffed animals. A small shrine. She wandered over to it, noticing that people had left tokens, rosaries, prayer cards, and even spare change. She read one of the faded cards that had been placed there: *Madison Lane, our angel, taken too soon.*

Inside, the place was bustling. She went to the back refrigerator case and got a cherry Gatorade, then headed to the check-out. The woman at the check-out was a middle-aged Hispanic lady with a bright smile. As Mia counted out her change for the drink, she said, "Did you know that girl? Madison Lane?"

The smile faded as she punched the buttons on the old register and the cash drawer sprang open. She clutched at her heart. "I did. My eldest boy went to school with her. So sad."

"She was from around here, huh?"

The woman nodded. "Lived right down the street from us. It was devastating for all of us. When she disappeared, we spent so much time looking for her. And then we got the news—" She patted her chest. "That her body was found. It was just the worst thing. Absolutely horrifying."

"Do you know if the police have any ideas about what might have happened to her?"

She shrugged. "None at all. Oh, there were rumors going around that she might've run away with an old boyfriend. But Pedro—that's my boy—he said she wasn't like that. She was a good girl, didn't really have any boyfriends. Stayed to herself, mostly. But nice. And very smart. They were in all the honors classes together."

"I read in the newspaper that she was missing for a long time."

"Months!" She shook her head. "Her poor family was going out of their minds with worry. And to find her body so close to home . . . it didn't make sense. Because we'd all searched that area, again and again. And the coroner even said that from the condition of her remains that she hadn't been dead long. So I have my own theories."

"You do?"

"I sure do." Another customer came with a hot dog and a soda. The cashier rang it up and collected the money, then leaned in to Mia. "Sex traffickers."

"Sex traffickers?"

She nodded. "This area is a hotbed for coyotes, bringing immigrants across the border. Hiding people is big business around here. The police are overwhelmed with it, so they do nothing. My feeling is that she got taken in by one of these slavers, who rented her out, then killed her when she wasn't useful anymore."

"Interesting," Mia said. It was plausible. "You heard about the other girl who was killed?"

The cashier shoved the cash drawer closed and nodded. "The girl from Waco? Yep. Another pretty young girl. I'm telling you. Sex traffickers."

"Thanks for the info," she said, backing away from the counter. Now, it made sense to tour where the bodies had been found. She'd been there before, but too long ago. None of this area was familiar. "Would you be able to point me in the direction of where the bodies were found. This Phantom Bridge?"

She pointed up the road, then narrowed her eyes in disgust. "What for? Are you one of those people who get a morbid fascination with visiting crime scenes?"

"No . . .," she said backing away. "I'm just a friend of the latest victim's family. Rachel Loring. And I was hoping I could get some answers."

The woman nodded. "All right. If you go up the road a bit, a couple miles, you'll see a sign for the place. If you get to Del Rio, you've gone too far. But there's nothing out there anymore, I'm afraid."

"I appreciate your help," she said, stepping outside. She took a drink of her Gatorade and hoisted her bag up on her shoulder. Sweat beaded on her brow. It was probably about a hundred degrees, even though the sun was setting, spreading its orange haze over the dark mountains in the distance.

It was definitely a mystery, where those girls had been kept, before their deaths. One she couldn't seem to shake out of her mind. Where had they gone? Had they run away, and been happy, at first? When had they realized they were in trouble? The questions and possible scenarios multiplied in her head. Sex-trafficking, running away, kidnapping . . . Mia felt sure there was a common thread among all three girls, and not just their appearance and the way they died. Something else. Something sinister.

She had to find a place to stay for the night, and Bracketville seemed like a good place—remote, quiet. If she turned left, towards downtown, there was probably a cheap motel where she could rent a room.

But she also wanted to see where these poor girls had met their ends. And that was what she could find if she turned right.

Thinking of that burning girl in her dream, she headed for the Phantom Bridge.

CHAPTER EIGHT

Just as the cashier had said, Mia found the sun-faded sign for Phantom Bridge about two miles up the road. When she arrived there, the sun was just setting behind the distant mountains. From there, she could see the lush line of vegetation that surrounded the Rio Grande.

The area was barren, scattered with dust and creosote bushes, just as she'd remembered. It was flat, the earth so dry that it had deep fissures crisscrossing it. It was a good place to dump a body, she decided, because no one would want to visit this place.

But there had been people there. As she wandered into the desert, carefully keeping her eyes trained for rattlesnakes, she found an abandoned car, old and decayed to a rusty carcass. She remembered all of this, but it wasn't any good to her.

She didn't have police photos or reports, and had no means of getting them. All she had was what she remembered from the Carrie Winters case, and that wasn't very much.

As Mia spun around, looking for some kind of clue, something glistened on the ground by the car.

At first, she thought it was a piece of broken glass from the windshield. But as she got closer, she noticed a bit of rubber tubing, a small glass bottle, and a couple hypodermic needles. She stooped and lifted one up. People had come out here to do drugs. Had the girls?

She peered inside the car, looking for more clues, but only found more needles, and some old fast-food wrappers and junk. Apparently, people had used this site frequently, though she was alone now.

She walked around the car, to the other side of it and noticed several footprints in the dust—male dress shoes, consistent with what the police or Border Patrol might wear. There was also some discarded police tape, hanging from one of the door handles. The dry creosote bushes in the area were black, showing definite signs of being scorched.

Was this where Rachel's body had been found? All signs pointed to it.

If so, it aligned with her memory of Carrie Winters. At the time, they'd gone out into the middle of a barren area, only to find a charred place where the burned body was found. She wasn't sure exactly where they'd found the body, but it had to have been close to this spot. She couldn't remember whether they'd found drug paraphernalia at the site, but the sense of déjà vu was strong. She could remember having similar questions—why would a girl come to this remote location? Who could she have been with? Did she know she was coming out there to die? Was she afraid?

Mia stepped away and shielded her eyes from the sun as she looked back toward the road. She could barely see it, in the distance.

No way would anyone have dragged a dead body all the way out here, just to set it on fire. It looked like Rachel had come out here on her own, and been murdered right at this spot.

The thought sent a shiver down Mia's back. If that was the case, then she had to wonder . . . who had Rachel been with? Had she been doing drugs? Had she come out here willingly? Or had she been fleeing her captor and wound up here, purely by chance?

Now that there had been more murders, the picture should have been clearer. It didn't seem like this was a chance occurrence, now. But that opened a whole other can of worms. Why would someone be killing young girls here?

More questions atop questions. She needed answers.

She cursed herself and pulled out her phone. If Marcus wanted help, he'd have to help her, too. Maybe she could get some more details on the case from him.

She groaned when she looked at the display on her phone. *No service.*

Made sense. This area was completely remote. She let out another curse and pocketed her phone. She'd have to work with what she already knew.

But it was getting dark. She had to get back to town.

As she walked along the highway, she thought hard, trying to remember details from the Carrie Winters case. As a new agent, she'd been a bit more apprehensive about making mistakes and ruffling feathers, so she probably hadn't turned over every stone she could have. Not to mention that she was new, and she'd learned a lot during her years on the job. The more experienced Mia probably would have dug a lot harder. There were a lot of things she hadn't done—like interviewing classmates at school or cross-checking with other area missing persons reports. At least, she didn't think she had—it'd been so long, and she'd had hundreds of cases since then. Without the files, how could she remember every detail?

It was better to generalize, she decided, as she continued toward town. She kept checking her phone. When she drew closer, her cell phone service returned. She dialed Marcus on the number he'd given her.

"Hey," he said, answering on the first ring.

"Hi. I'm just calling you, because I wanted you to know that I'm—"

"Near Bracketville. I've got it."

She sighed. So much for being a master of disguise, slipping in and out of places unnoticed. "You're tracking me."

"Hey. That's what I do. Hold on." There was a long pause, a sound of things moving around, and then, "Sorry. I had to get out of earshot."

"Where are you?"

"At the office. I'm working late on a case," he said, his voice so low she could barely hear him. "Listen. It's not a good idea that you call me. At all. Ever. There's this Marshal, asking all these—"

"I know. I know."

"Then you'll know why you can't call me."

"Yes, but Marcus. I don't know what you expect me to get done. I don't have any files. The case we investigated was eight years ago. I barely remember it. I'm here, but I have nothing to go o—"

"Come on, Mia. You're resourceful. You can find something. I know you can."

She opened her mouth, but nothing came out. She wished she could share his faith in her. "Marcus—"

"Please, Mia. Just do your best. I've got to go."

And then there was nothing but dead air.

She growled a curse and tucked her phone in her pocket. *Sure, Marcus, no problem, I'll just pull our murderer out of thin air. What does he think I am, a magician?*

The sun was just about down as she reached the edge of town and found a Motel 6. As she approached, she was trying to think back to what she knew about most missing persons cases. She knew the vast majority of the women who went missing had something else going on in their lives—mental illness, domestic violence, drug-related activity.

She'd nearly reached the motel lobby when a voice called, "Hey."

Mia looked up to see a man, stepping out of the shadows. Though his face was young, he had a massively receding hairline, and was smoking a cigarette as he leaned against the wall.

"Me?"

He nodded. "Yeah. You. You looking for a room?"

"Yes . . ." The hairs on the back of Mia's neck stood up.

"Maybe a little fun?" He winked.

"Definitely not." She took a step away.

"Aw, come on. Want to stay for free?"

"What?"

"I'm just sayin'. If cash is a little tight, you come on to Mario here. I'll help you out. Out of the goodness of my heart."

Sure. Did people really buy that line? Maybe. Desperate women probably did, ones who had no other choice.

She held up a hand. She had a very good idea of what he'd want in return. "I don't think so. I—"

"Come on, girl. Party with me." He opened one side of his army jacket to reveal a giant stash of what looked like heroin.

Mia looked down at herself. Did she look like a drug addict? Probably. She hadn't showered in a couple days, she was dirty, sweaty, and tired, and all she had to her name was an old backpack. "Thanks, but I don't do that stuff," she said, pulling on the door.

"Aw, you're no fun!"

"Exactly."

"If you change your mind, I'm in Room One," he called to her, sauntering away.

A bell jingled as Mia walked in, but that didn't bring the manager. Mia was happy to see the prominent CASH ONLY sign at the reception desk. She looked around, and was about to hit the bell on the desk when she noticed a form, sitting in the back room, pale legs propped up on an ottoman.

The old, large woman in a flowered housecoat didn't even get up from the couch there. Judging from the canned laughter, she was watching some sit-com. "My knee's no good. It's too hard for me to get up. Just leave forty bucks on the counter," she said, tapping the black brace on her doughy leg. "You can have number twelve. Key's on a hook over there. Just do me a favor and reach over and grab it, all right, honey?"

Mia set down a couple of twenties, reached over the desk, and grabbed her key from a peg. Judging from the peg board, all of the rooms were vacant, except hers and number one. "Thank you," she said, able to get a better look at the woman from that vantage point. She had a number of chins and thin, blonde, stringy hair in a low ponytail resting on her shoulder.

"No problem, honey. Grab yourself a couple of snacks on the way out. If there're any left, throw me an Oreo, would you?"

Mia found the complimentary refreshment service next to the picture window looking out onto the parking lot. A couple of flies buzzed near it, half-interested in the food, half interested in the dying sunlight filtering through the window. Though the hotel didn't appear to have many customers, people had definitely taken advantage of the free snacks. The table was dirty, with coffee stains and spilled sugar and used stirrers and napkins everywhere, but what it did have was an entire sleeve of slightly-broken Oreos, and about half a tin of Danish butter cookies. She grabbed a couple of the sandwich cookies and wrapped them in a napkin, then held them up to the woman. "Here you go."

She held up a doughy arm and wiggled her fingers. "Throw. I'll catch."

Mia was doubtful. Her throw went a little wide, but impressively, the woman snatched it out of the air. She was deceptively fast for her size. "Thanks, honey. You have a great night and let me know if you need anything, all right?"

Mia nodded, grabbing a Styrofoam cup of coffee and a few butter cookies from the table and headed to her room. By the time she got to it, at the very end of the strip of a dozen rooms, the creepy drug guy was gone.

She went inside. The room was stuck in the seventies, with shag carpet and paneled walls, and it smelled like something had died. But whatever. She'd stayed at worse places. And, like all the places she rested her head, it was only temporary. She'd have to move on.

She threw her bag down, looked around, and yawned.

She sat on the edge of a sunflower-covered comforter, thinking about poor Rachel Loring.

Marcus had said she was such a good girl, but he didn't know her secrets. She probably hid them from her family.

Mia wasn't sure about mental illness or domestic violence, but after finding the drug paraphernalia at that old car, she zoned in on the possibility of drug use.

She stood up. If the girls were using drugs, she had a good idea where she could start.

CHAPTER NINE

Five minutes later, the sun had fully set. Mia poked her head out, finding it completely dark except for the flashing VACANCY sign in the distance. All of the nearby streetlights seemed to be out.

Right about now, if she was home, she'd be telling Kelsey to get up and ready for bed. Kelsey would complain, saying she wanted more snuggles, but Mia would be adamant, finally having to pry her daughter's arms off her and send her into the bathroom to brush her teeth.

Now, she would've given anything for another snuggle from her little girl. It felt like eons since she'd been able to do that.

She shook off the memories that threatened to turn her into a sobbing mess. She had work to do.

The desert air had already turned chilly. As she took a step out, a gunshot went off nearby. Her first instinct, to hide, was quickly squelched when she heard a number of voices raised in anger. It sounded like it was coming from down the street, closer to the center of town.

She already knew that this probably wasn't the safest area of town, but that was okay. In order to swallow the mouse, sometimes you had to crawl on the ground with the snakes. If anyone knew who was responsible for Rachel Loring's murder, she had a good feeling she'd find the answers here.

Mia walked down the row of motel rooms, to number one. She knocked.

A second later, the skinny man with the receding hairline answered. Now, he was wearing a dirty undershirt, and a shock of his oily hair was standing up on end. He studied her from head to toe, a lascivious smile widening on his face. "So . . . you changed your mind, huh? Come on in."

"No, I didn't. I have questions."

His smile faded. He started to close the door. "One thing I don't got is answers."

She stuck her foot in, wedging it open. "I think you do."

He snorted and pushed on the door. "You can't make me tell you anything."

"I bet I can," she said, removing the gun from her pocket and pointing it at him.

His expression wasn't one of fear, more like annoyance. "What the hell?" He sighed, poked his head out, and looked up and down the empty street. "Fine. Come in."

She hesitated.

"Come in, will you?" He shoved the door open so she could enter. "If I'm going to tell you something, I'm not going to do it out in the open. There are people out there who'll have my head, if you know what I mean."

She stepped inside, still pointing the gun at him, and closed the door.

His room had the same unpleasant décor as hers, but this one was even worse. It was littered with fast food wrappers, newspapers, magazines, and assorted other trash, and both double beds were unmade. It smelled like old grease and cigarettes. She fought the urge to gag as he went to the table near the window and stubbed out his cigarette in an ashtray.

"Didn't think you'd be packing, girl. Of course, you're older than my usual clientele. And you look like you've been around the block a time or two." He grinned. "So what's this about? You looking for Rico?"

"Who's Rico?" she asked, not moving from her place, a few inches from the door.

He laughed at her. "You can relax. I'm not armed. I ain't gonna hurt you. In case you didn't notice, I'm not the one with the gun," he said with a laugh. When she didn't move, he shrugged. "Rico's the big daddy around here. The one everyone knows. That you don't know him tells me that you're not from around here. Where you from, baby?"

"Where can I find him?"

He laughed more. "You don't find Rico. Rico finds you. Him and his guys. Trust me, he has enough of them. They own the streets. They own this place. You found the camera in your room, huh?"

She blinked. "What?"

He laughed. "And here I thought you were a smart one. Forget it."

"What's the camera for?"

"Nothing. Just—"

She shoved the gun in his face. "Tell me. Why are you spying on people?"

"No. Cameras feed into the main office. The manager waits for you to fall asleep and then sends me to look through your stuff. Anything we find, we split, fifty-fifty."

"With Rico?"

"No, that's small shit for him. But he keeps tabs on all the girls passing through here. He likes to keep his inventory circulating."

"Is he the one who supplied you with the drugs?"

He nodded. "You can get drugs anywhere around here. They come right over the border. Rico's the biggest operation, and most others are afraid to step in on his business. But you didn't hear it from me. Yeah. I sell for him. But I'm one of a dozen in this town. I'm small potatoes compared to some of the others."

"You have to know where I can find him."

He tapped another cigarette out, sat back on the edge of a bed, and started to light it. "I don't. I swear, I don't."

"You know anything about Rachel Loring?"

His gaze shot to hers. "Who?"

"Loring. The girl whose body was found at Phantom Bridge a few days ago."

He hitched a shoulder. "I might."

She pushed the gun closer to him. "Don't give me that shit. What do you know?"

"Easy, easy," he said, shaking his head. "Sheesh, you're high-strung. What are you, a cop?"

Her hard expression didn't falter. "I'm a friend of the family."

He shook his head. "I don't know nothin' for certain. But there's a guy. Drives a beaten red pick-up and comes to town every week or so. He's my best customer. He loads up on drugs, more drugs than any one guy can consume on his own. Brings in a lot of girls, too. So one day, a couple months ago, I ask him what he's up to, and he said he likes to party with girls outside of town. He invited me once. So I went. It was Phantom Bridge."

"And what happened?"

"It was like he said," he said, sucking on his cigarette. "There were girls there, and they were shootin' up, but it wasn't my scene. The girls were too young for me. I got standards, you know?"

She raised an eyebrow. He did? "So you left?"

"I left. But that was months ago. When I heard about those girls being found around here, about a month later and then a few days ago, I wondered if it was him."

"Do you have his name?"

He scratched his temple. "He goes by the name of Coop. But I don't know if that's his real name. We don't use names around here. But I think he has something going on with Sue, so I'd ask her. He always stopped in to see her after he saw me."

"Sue?"

He pointed. "Woman in the office. The manager."

It wasn't much. Maybe it wasn't anything. But it was something to go on. She relaxed her gun and reached for the door. "Thank you. That's what I needed."

He held up a packet. "Sure you don't want to? This is some damn good stuff, if I do say so myself."

"I thought you said you didn't do that stuff?"

He shrugged and fixed her with what he must've thought was his most charming smolder. Whatever effect he was hoping to have, it actually had the opposite. "On special occasions, I'll make an exception. So, you in?"

"No," she said flatly, stepping outside. "And if you try going through my stuff tonight, mark my words. I'll break your wrist."

She left him, staring wide-eyed after her. But she had more important things to deal with. She had to get to the office and follow this lead.

CHAPTER TEN

A moment later, she was back in the motel office. The bells overhead tinkled as she walked in, but unsurprisingly, there was no greeting.

The back-office manager hadn't moved from her place on the sofa. It sounded like the television was now onto some news program. "Leave forty dollars on the counter. You can have room six," she muttered.

"It's me. I just checked into room twelve, remember?" she said, leaning over the counter and waving.

The woman had cookie crumbs all over her enormous chest. Her eyes went up to the ceiling.

"Honey," she mumbled, her eyes trailing back to the television screen. "If you need more towels, I haven't got any yet. The service isn't due back until tomorrow morning."

"That's not what I'm here for. I need information."

The woman shook her head. "If you want local tourist attractions, I can't help you. There ain't nothing worth seeing around here, anymore. Check out the brochure rack if you don't believe me," she said, shifting the pillow behind her large frame.

Mia glanced at the small, unkempt brochure rack, stuffed with dog-eared, sun-faded attraction brochures. Most of the stuff advertised was paintball and all-you-can-eat buffets. Not that Mia was interested in any of that.

"Hey, honey, while you're out there, can you get me some more cookies?"

"None left," Mia said, pushing open the half-door and stepping behind the counter. "And I need to talk to you."

The woman's eyes widened in alarm. "What are you—you're not supposed to be back here! I'll call the—"

"Sue," she said, leaning against the door frame. From here, she could clearly see the local news reporter on the television screen. Mia hoped that the news of her escape wasn't a big headline around here. "Where's the camera in my room?"

Her eyes narrowed. "Who told you that? There's no--"

"And I suppose this closed-caption television set is an episode of *Gilligan's Island,*" she snapped, reaching over and turning it on. Sure enough, it showed a darkened image of a shabby hotel room, from above.

The woman said, "It's for security. Too many people doing drugs."

Mia snorted. "Give it up. The guy outside told me the little scheme you have going on with him."

Her face reddened. "I don't know what you're talking about."

"Don't give me that. He told me what you two were up to."

She sighed. "Ah, Luther! He's such a little scumbag. I let him stay here for free out of the goodness of my heart, and this is how he repays me."

"You let him stay there so that he can get people high and rob them while they're sleeping."

Her lips twisted. Then she pointed to her knee. "I'm an invalid. I can't do much. I don't know what he's up to, but I'm innocent. If he told you otherwise, he's a liar."

Mia paced the floor and shook her head. "That's bullshit."

Sue scowled. "What are you, a police officer?"

"No. I'm just someone who wants answers. And if you don't want me to turn you in for this little scheme you've been playing with your customers, you'd better start talking."

She pressed her lips together. "Answers about what?"

"About Rachel Loring, the girl who was murdered outside of town a few days ago."

She shrugged. "I saw on the news that a girl died. That's all. I don't know nothing else about it."

"Luther says that you do. He says that there's a drifter who he said liked to party with girls outside of town, in Phantom Bridge, where the girl's body was found. Goes by the name of Coop?"

She was already shaking her head, but something about the way she averted her eyes told Mia that Sue wasn't telling the whole truth. "It doesn't ring a bell."

"Funny. Luther says every time he came here, he stopped in to see you."

She slammed a fat hand down on the wooded arm of the sofa. "Damn, that Luther! I never should have agreed to anything with him. He's such an idiot."

"So you *do* know Coop?"

"I might. But I haven't seen him in a while." More averting her eyes. More lying.

"Luther said you saw him just a few days ago. Right before Rachel was killed," she said. It was a lie—Luther hadn't said that— but she hoped it might get Sue to admit it.

She sighed and shook her head. "Yeah. All right. I suppose it was just a few days ago. But I have no idea where he was going or what he was up to. I swear on that."

"You must know where he hangs out?"

She shook her head. "He's a drifter. Never in one place very long. I try to keep him home and out of trouble but he finds it, all the time."

"Home?" Mia asked, confused.

Sue put her head back and stared at the ceiling. She took a deep breath in, then let it out. "He's my son."

Well, now it made sense, why she was trying to protect him. "You know that your son might be implicated in the murder of Rachel Loring?"

She motioned to the television. "Of course I did. I seen on the television. But I don't believe he'd do that. Set that girl on fire like that. If you're looking for the person who did that to her, you've got the wrong man."

Of course she'd say that, of her son. "Yeah, well—I still need to find him."

She looked around, her brow wrinkled in concentration. "Why?"

"I made a promise to the Loring family. And if he's been known for drifting around these places, then maybe he's seen her."

She nodded. "I suppose. I know he's not been the best of kids and he's gotten into his share of trouble with drugs and drinking, but that's not the boy I raised. I worry about him. If you can find him, maybe you can talk some sense into him? One day, I'm afraid he's going to get himself killed."

Mia shrugged. She had enough to deal with in her life—convincing a thug to give up his life of crime was pretty low on her list. "I'll try. Do you have any idea where he might be right now?"

She nodded. "Fort Alamo."

Mia frowned. "You mean that he's all the way in San Antonio?"

"No, no. Fort Alamo. The replica that was built outside of town for that John Wayne film. Can you imagine if they tried to film that movie in the real Alamo? It's in the middle of a city! Anyway, ours was a tourist attraction, where all the westerns were made in Texas—"

"I thought you said that there were no tourist attractions around here?"

"There aren't," she said huffily. "The village closed down a few years back, and now all the drifters and snowbirds flock that way to camp out there."

"Oh. All right. Where is it in relation to Phantom Bridge?"

"About twenty miles away. You head out of town on the Texas Pecos Trail going north, and you can't miss it. You'll see all the tents and RVs parked there." She motioned out to the lobby. "There should be an old brochure for it, on the rack."

Mia went to the rack and found the brochure right away among the dusty pamphlets. She pulled it up and saw a photograph of John Wayne. It said:

Alamo Village is Texas's first permanent outdoor movie location and was built for John Wayne's epic "The Alamo." It sits in the middle of the18,000-acre Shahan HV Ranch, seven miles north of Brackettville on Hwy 674. The set, largest and most complete in the U.S., boasts a full-scale period town and the only replica of the 1836 Alamo mission in the world.

The Alamo and town were constructed with a dedication to authenticity. Our versatile sets, all full-scale buildings; no false fronts, include nearly three dozen board-and-batten and adobe buildings such as jails, saloons, general store, bank, hotel, church, stable, blacksmith shop, in addition to the Alamo mission-fortress.

Seven miles? She could walk it, but she wouldn't like it. Maybe she could hitch a ride.

Sue called, "If you go, be careful—it can get a little rough there. It's lawless. The people here ain't even supposed to be there—the police should arrest them. I wouldn't go at night."

"I'll go tomorrow, thank you." She made a motion to leave, and then stopped. "Hey, do me a favor. Can you tell me exactly where that camera you put in room twelve is?"

CHAPTER ELEVEN

The following morning, Mia headed out on foot up 674, otherwise known as the Texas Pecos Trail, in search for the old Alamo Village, hoping she could hitch a ride.

As she was walking, thumb out, she saw a couple of Border Patrol vehicles out in the fields.

Great. Feds.

Squinting in the bright sunlight, she shielded her eyes with her hand and scanned the area for their familiar green uniforms. She didn't see them. Mia had met a few friends in the Border Patrol while in training, so she knew that they were short-staffed, considering the amount of land they had to cover. Many of them just sat on an X, watching the U.S./Mexico border, all day, while sometimes, they just left a truck out there, which was often enough of a deterrent.

She couldn't see anybody in the driver's seat. It was just a truck.

She sighed with relief and held out a thumb for the next truck that passed. It was an old-model Ford with peeling paint. She smiled when its brake-lights flashed and it pulled over to the side.

The person driving it had a number of empty dog kennels in the back. She jogged up to the passenger-side window to find a young, gum-popping girl with a long dark braid down her back. Her radio was blasting Justin Bieber. "Hey, chica, where you going? Can I give you a ride? We girls have to stick together, you know?"

Mia smiled and got in. "Thanks, I just need a ride down the street, to the Alamo Village?"

The girl winced. "You sure? Why do you want to go there?"

"I'm just trying to learn more about the area. Are you from here?"

The girl blew a bubble and nodded. "Born and raised. My mama used to work at that Village. She used to be a ticket taker. Sad thing that happened to it. The owners died of old age. They hoped to sell it but there were no buyers. It closed down. Now it's falling apart. And now—with the vandals? Ay."

"Vandals?"

"Yeah. They broke down the gate and they moved in, and now the police don't even say anything. Tearing the place to ruin. If you go there, I'd watch my back. What could you possibly want to find there?"

"I'm looking for someone."

She made a face. "The type of people that live there . . . scare me."

"I think the person I'm looking for is probably a very scary person," she admitted, hooking her arm out the window and staring out at the stretch of barren desert. The hot air blew, like a hair dryer at high speed, right into her face.

"Really?" She turned the radio down. "Why?"

"You heard of the women that have been murdered outside of town?"

The girl nodded. "Yes, we all have. Phantom Bridge has always been haunted, though. You couldn't pay me to go out there. In high school, that was the big dare, to go out there at night." She laughed. "I'm a scaredy-cat. You couldn't pay me enough to go there."

Mia smiled sadly.

The girl sobered. "But what does that have to do with Alamo Village?"

"I'm a friend of one of the girls who was killed. And I'm looking for answers. I think someone in the village might be able to provide them to me."

"Ah," she said, pulling to the side of the road. There was nothing more than another dirt road, cutting through the brush and mesquite. There was a sign, too, but it was so battered by the sun that Mia couldn't read it. The girl motioned. "There it is."

The dust cleared, but nothing more came into view. It looked deserted. "Up that way?"

"Yep. If you stay to the left. Good luck."

Mia thanked the girl, opened the door, and got out. Feeling for the gun in her pocket, she walked up the curving, rutted dirt road, looking for any sign of civilization. Just as the girl promised, about a half-mile from the road, she saw it—a tent city, stretched out among a number of old, decaying stone buildings.

As she walked down the middle of the village, people stuck their heads out, but no one spoke to her. Most just sealed themselves back inside their tents. She almost felt like the hero in an old Western, visiting a city that's been so plagued by bandits, the residents had to hide themselves inside.

She read a sign that said, *Welcome to Alamo Village, where Texas Movies are Made!* There was a faded picture of a smiling man in a cowboy hat who had to be John Wayne. She walked toward an empty saloon, past the front of the old Alamo itself, noticing it was little more than a movie façade.

On cue, an actual tumbleweed bounced across the dirt road.

"Hey, what are you doing here?" a voice said behind her.

It was an old man with a white, unkempt beard, and a beaten Bass Pro Shops trucker's cap. He shook his head. "This campsite's full. We're not taking any more of Rico's rejects."

"I'm not looking to camp here. And I don't even know who Rico is."

"Eh?" he said, stroking his beard. "That a fact? Well, that's a miracle. So many girls land here after he gets done with 'em, I just assumed. At first, this was a great little place to stop. Now it's a shithole. Too many people. If you know what's good for you, you'll keep on walking."

"I won't stay. But I'm looking for someone. Someone named Coop."

The disgust on his face was palpable. "So that's what you're after. He's the one who ruined this place. Him and Rico. With the drugs. He stays over there. But you better have a good reason to be bothering him."

His finger stretched toward the old Alamo.

She followed it toward the entrance to the fort replica. When she went inside, it was easy to see around the place. Because it didn't have a roof, it was like an open courtyard. Dirty people were huddled against all the walls. Some were shaking; one was shooting up. They all ignored her. She watched all this with mild shock, then asked the one person who seemed to notice her presence, "Coop?"

He pointed to a door at the far end of the courtyard.

She walked over to it, navigating around creosote bushes and towels spread with people, curled into balls, rocking back and forth, looking generally hopeless. When she reached the door, she found it wide open. Her adrenaline spiked as she felt for the gun at her hip.

"Go away!" a voice from inside grouched. "I told you, I'm not making another run until tomorrow, so you're just going to have to deal with it!"

A young man with a long black beard and dirty corduroy pants that were hanging dangerously low on his slim frame emerged from the darkness. He was tall, so tall that he had to stoop to avoid hitting his head on the low ceiling. He approached the door, about to close it, stopping when he saw her. "Coop?" she asked.

He scowled. "Who the hell are you?"

"I don't want your drugs," she said, stepping in and crossing her arms. "I want answers."

He laughed. "You know where you are, don't you?" He motioned out to the courtyard. "You're in a place where no one gives a shit who anyone else is, and where everyone just wants to be left alone. Including me."

He reached for the door.

"I spoke to your mother," she said.

He hesitated. "So? What, is she trying to stage an intervention or something? I told her, I'm not an addict like these people. I provide a service. That's all."

"What do you get in return for that serv—"

"Coop?" a female voice called from behind him.

Oh, well, there was the reason. He probably had plenty of female attention, now, as a supplier of drugs, and lord over this city. But she really didn't care about that, unless one of them was Rachel Loring. "Look. I'm looking for someone. A girl. And I need your help."

He shook his head. "Sorry. I know too many girls. And I don't ask for their life histories. I'm all over the place around this county, and I can barely remember who I was with last night. Sorry."

He started to close the door.

"You'd remember this one, since she's dead," Mia said flatly.

He stopped. "You mean Rachel."

She blinked in surprise. "Yes. Yes, do you know her?"

"Are you police?"

"Do I look like police? I'm just a concerned friend."

He looked back into the room, then muttered that he'd be right back to whoever was inside, came out, and closed the door. "Walk with me."

She followed him through an opening in the courtyard, to what looked like the back of an eating establishment, with old picnic tables that had been reduced to little more than firewood. He sat on one of them and motioned to her to sit across from him. Then he drummed his fingers nervously in front of him.

"Yeah. I know her. I expected the police would try to catch up with me eventually and ask me about her. So let's get one thing straight. I ain't got nothing to hide regarding her. I'm innocent."

"Were you out with her at Phantom Bridge?"

He shook his head.

"I've heard otherwise."

His eyes narrowed. "Who—"

"Someone named Luther."

He sucked in a breath, let it out. "All right. Fine. It was a few months ago. There were a couple girls, and they were new in town. So I took them out to this place in the desert, where we wouldn't be bothered, and we'd party. I've done it a lot of times."

"And then?"

"And then . . . nothing. We went our separate ways." He shrugged. He looked like he was holding something back, though. "I didn't think anything of it until I saw her picture in the paper. And then I found out her body was left around the same place where I had my parties. And I knew it looked bad for me. But I swear to you, I didn't touch her. She left that morning."

"Do you know where she was headed?"

He eyed her, then shook his head slowly. "No . . . I can't . . ." His eyes lit up. "Wait. She said she was going to the Rising Sun. I remember that. She said she'd heard about it on the internet and her family was giving her shit and she just wanted to get away."

Rising Sun. Now why does that name sound familiar? "The Rising Sun?"

"Yeah. It's a commune. It's even more remote than this shithole, if you can believe it. West of here. You can't get there by car. Only by foot."

"A commune . . ."

"Yeah. They grow food and live together and help each other out. Rachel said it sounded like heaven, being part of a family who 'cared,' because most of her family only wanted to give her grief about her future. I told her about how those places make you drink the Kool-Aid and shave your heads, but I couldn't talk her out of it. She thought it sounded like heaven." He drummed his fingers some more. "A shame. She was a really pretty, really nice girl."

Suddenly, the long disappearance of these girls seemed to make sense. If Rachel and the others had gone out to this commune, then maybe they'd been living there for a while before their deaths.

The question was, what happened after that in order to result in their deaths?

"Can you point me the direction of Rising Sun, then?" she asked.

He shook his head. "All I know is that it's west of here, and hard to get to. Somewhere in the foothills of the Sierra Madres, I think." He motioned to the gently sloping, brown mountains in the distance. "Like I said, I don't believe in that stuff. Creeps me out. So I never looked for it. And I don't think those people want to be found."

"Well, thanks," she said, rising from the bench. She'd have to find a way to get there, somehow.

CHAPTER TWELVE

David Hunter sat at the kitchen table that morning, trying to enjoy his first mug of fresh-brewed coffee.

Thunk. Crash.

The men upstairs would never qualify as cat burglars. They were destroying the upstairs of his house, just as they'd done to the downstairs, yesterday.

He thought about what US Marshal Kane Wilcox had said to him. *If we find so much as a post-it note, tying you to Mia, your ass is grass.*

Unbelievable.

Across the table from him, his son Louie was scooping Cheerios into his mouth, eyes wide with worry. "Dad," he said between chews. "They're in my room."

He managed a smile. "I know, kid. But they won't mess with anything."

At least, he hoped not. He understood their thinking—if he was going to keep evidence about his connection to Mia, he wouldn't keep it out in the open, or in his own room. He'd keep it in the most inconspicuous place. Like Louie's room. But they'd been going through everything, leaving no stone unturned. Yesterday, they'd put things in bags—a notebook from his desk, an old Kindle reader he hadn't touched since 2018, the comforter from his bed—and toted it all out of the house.

The comforter from his bed? That was a new one. He wasn't sure what the hell they expected to extract from that one.

But even though he was fairly sure they wouldn't find anything tying him to her, it was still unnerving, having cops rummaging through his private things.

Not to mention that this was the first time in his life that he was hiding something huge from everyone he knew—his boss, his family, everyone who mattered to him. He'd been walking on eggshells for a long time, and the stress was starting to hurt. He could feel cracks forming in his calm façade. People were starting to notice.

Louie, especially. He was a perceptive kid. And now, he looked absolutely terrified. No wonder.

"Look, it'll be over soon," he said reassuringly, his hand running over the pocket of his jacket, where he'd kept his burner phone and the gun.

He couldn't keep them on his person. It was only a matter of time before Pembroke ordered them to search him. He'd need to hide them, somewhere. Today, as soon as he dropped Louie off at the bus stop, he'd find a place. He'd been thinking of good, safe, out-of-the-way places to meet Mia, all along. It wouldn't be hard to find a place to stash this stuff.

"But what are they doing this for?" he asked, rubbing his nose. "Does this have anything to do with your partner?"

He blinked. He'd always tried to keep Louie separate from his business. That was the first time he'd ever asked about Mia. "What do you know about that?"

"Dad. Everyone at school asks me about it, all the time. I heard she was a dirty FBI agent, doing bad things. Do they think you are one, too?"

He shook his head. "No. No, they don't," he said, the lie tasting bitter on his tongue. "You know how I always tell you to pick up your room and finish your homework Friday night, even when no one's coming over and your homework isn't technically due on Monday? Well, same thing here. They're just doing it because that's the way things are done. Not because I'm in trouble."

Louie gazed at him doubtfully. "If they touch my baseball card collection, I'm going to kick their butts," he whispered.

"I'm sure they'll leave everything the way they found it."

"They didn't, down here," he mumbled. "They left a big mess in my man cave."

He snorted. "*Your* man cave is actually the playroom, and you do enough of messing up that place on your own. If I have to tell you to pick up those Legos one more time . . ."

Louie rolled his eyes and scooped more Cheerios into his mouth.

David's coffee was now cold. He dumped it out and grabbed Louie's cereal bowl after he got the last mouthful, then put it in the sink. "Get ready, we're running late."

He went to the foot of the stairs, where he listened and realized they were now in the guest bedroom.

"Hey," he called up the stairs to them. "I'm heading out to take my kid to school and run a couple errands. I'll be back in an hour."

"You got it!" Ellis, the lead officer on the case, replied cheerfully. He was trying to make this as pleasant for Hunter as possible, which Hunter appreciated, but it was still damn awkward, watching the men go through his stuff.

He found his son hovering next to him, looking up the stairs. "What's up? Go. Brush your teeth."

He wrinkled his nose. "I don't wanna. Not with them up there."

"All right. Fine. Use the downstairs bathroom."

"But all I got down here is my old, gross toothbrush—"

"I guess you've got a decision to make, then. Just make it or you'll miss your bus."

Head down, he trudged into the downstairs bathroom. He returned about ten seconds later, which made David wonder how well he'd brushed those teeth. He handed Louie his backpack and the two of them went out to the car, parked in his driveway.

The two police cars parked in front of his house added *real* curb appeal. He already got his share of glances from being the only African-American family in the neighborhood. Didn't matter how often he mowed his lawn or how neat he kept the place—people always looked twice. They were friendly enough, but distant. He'd never been invited over to a block barbecue. He could only imagine what his neighbors were thinking now.

As they were driving, Louie was quiet. There was no doubt he was thinking about the police, swarming their house. David said, "Thinking about that game this weekend, huh?" mostly to distract him. "You're going to do great."

It didn't work. Louie said, "Savannah at school told me that Mia's on the FBI Ten Most Wanted List. Is that true?"

David shook his head. "No. She's not. She's going through stuff, yeah."

"She's your friend."

"Yeah."

"Did she really do all those things they say she did?"

David shook his head. "I don't think so."

"So you are helping her?" His eyes were wide. "Because if everyone thought I did something, and I didn't, I'd want someone to be on my side."

"I'm on her side. But it's not as simple as me telling people I don't think she did it. We have to have evidence. Until then, there's not much I can do."

"Are you looking for it?"

"Look, kid," he said with a sad smile. "There are things you want to do, right? Like play baseball all day, and forget about school? But you have rules you have to follow. Unfortunately, so do I. So it's not that easy. I'm doing what I can."

David pulled his car up to the curb, where a number of other elementary school kids were waiting, some with their parents. As he stopped, Louie turned to him. "Dad, you're not going to get arrested like she was, are you?"

"No. That's not going to happen," he said, squeezing his son's bony shoulder. "Don't worry about that."

"Okay, Dad," he said, smiling. "Love you."

He hopped out of the car and joined a bunch of his friends at the bus stop. David watched him go, his stomach feeling queasy. *At least, I hope I don't do anything stupid enough to get myself arrested.*

Which gave him all the more reason to get rid of the evidence on his person.

*

He drove outside of town, checking every so often to make sure he wasn't being followed. On the outskirts of town, he came to the grounds of an old one-room elementary school that had been abandoned, years ago. As he drove up the driveway toward it, he checked in his rear-view mirror, just to be sure.

Then he got out of the car, went to the front doors, and looked around for a hiding place. He found it in a line of stones, surrounding the pathway. Prying the third one from the door up, he hollowed out a space in the earth there with his fingers. Then he grabbed the bag with the gun and the phone from his pocket, and buried it under the rock.

He stared at it for a moment, then looked around again to make sure he was alone.

Dammit. He'd let the battery on the phone drain, so he had no idea where she was. He hadn't spoken to her since she asked him to get the gun, and the last text said that she didn't need it. He wished he'd been able to ask what she was up to. But now, it was too dangerous. The best he could do was lie low, keep the stuff stashed, and wait for all this to blow over.

Yes, he decided as he got back in the car. It was a very good thing that he had no idea where Mia North was, now.

When he returned to his house, surprisingly, the two police cars were gone. He wondered if they'd gotten all they needed, or if they'd be back to continue the search. As he climbed the steps and went inside, he also wondered if they'd done something more than just search. As an FBI agent, he knew their tactics.

And he knew they could've bugged the place.

He scanned the area, thinking about places where he'd be most likely to plant a bug. Curiously, he went to a lamp and peered in the lamp shade. Nothing.

Then he climbed up the stairs, trying to see if they'd taken anything else with them. On first glance, nothing appeared to be missing. He thought he saw something a little strange behind the antique mirror above his bed, and was just climbing up to check it when the doorbell rang.

I guess it was just wishful thinking to hope that this nightmare would be over, he thought, jumping off the bed and jogging downstairs.

He'd suspected it was the police again, and he wasn't wrong. But it wasn't the team who'd been here earlier.

No, standing in front of him was a heavy-set woman with white-blonde hair and a neat uniform. The brass nameplate on her breast said, *Clopecki.*

David Hunter had come to know a lot about Mia North during their three years as partners. Even little things, like her maiden name. And once upon a time, years ago, when he was new to the force, he'd come to a family barbecue at her house, and met her entire family.

This woman had Mia North's eyes, too.

"Francine?" he asked, the name springing into his mind.

"That's right," she said with a fragile smile. She had a softer, quieter demeanor than her sister. From what he remembered, she worked the front desk at another precinct in Dallas, and had only joined the force because it was what her father had done. "May I come in?"

He didn't want to be rude, but he had a feeling, whatever she was going to have to say, the Marshals would be very interested in it. He stepped out and closed the door behind him. "Why don't you and I take a walk?"

She raised an eyebrow. "You mean . . ." She mouthed the word, *Bugs?*

"Yeah," he said, leading her down the driveway. "Well, I don't know for sure, but better to be safe than sorry. The police were just here, searching."

"For what?"

He shrugged. "Anything. Really. They're grasping at straws. They don't have anything to go on. But the Marshals are involved. Have they come to you at all?"

She shook her head. "Well, once, when this first started. They asked a few questions, but the whole interview took no more than five minutes. You know, where I thought she might have gone and if we had any family or friends she might be getting help from. Of course, I told them nothing, because I didn't know anything. I think Mia did that on purpose. But I'm surprised. I thought they'd be back."

"Me too. Not only are they not leaving any stone unturned, but they seem to want to *keep* turning them, over and over again."

They reached the end of the block on his tree-lined street and rounded a corner. He looked up and saw one of his elderly neighbors, standing on her porch, watching them with hawkish eyes.

Francine noticed too, and hugged herself. "It hasn't been easy for you, has it?"

"I don't think it's been easy for any of us. When was the last time you spoke with her?"

"A long time ago. I tried to visit but she wouldn't see me. She never called, and she wouldn't take my phone calls. I think she was trying to protect me and our parents," she said with a shake of her head. "The last time I spoke to her, she told me that the charges were false and she was being set up. Did she tell you that?"

"Yes. She did."

"But she didn't say who was setting her up. Did she tell you that?"

"I think if she knew that, she'd probably be walking free by now."

She stopped and stared straight into his eyes. "Mr. Hunter . . . tell me, do you think that Mia is guilty?"

He shook his head immediately. "No. I don't."

"I'm glad. Because Mia has always been stubbornly independent. She hates to ask for help, especially if she knows it'll put a person out. I get the feeling she wouldn't accept help from me, even if I dangled it out in front of her. But I can help. I want to." She hugged herself tighter. "But I have no idea how to get in touch with her. Do you?"

Hunter stared at her, hesitating. Yes, she was Mia's sister. But he didn't know her well. And he wasn't sure if he could trust her. What if the chief had sent her here, hoping to get the dirt on Mia's whereabouts? "I don't, no," he finally said. "I don't know where she is. She could be anywhere, really, by now."

As much as he hated to say it, it was the truth.

"That's too bad," she said, sighing. "I just wish I could tell her, she's not alone. We're all here, and we believe her. It's driving my parents crazy, not knowing if she's okay."

"I'm sure she's okay. Mia's a fighter," he said. "A survivor. I have no doubt that wherever she is, she's working like hell to get home to her family."

"I think you're right, but I'd like to help her. In any way I can."

They'd rounded the block, and now his house was in sight again. When they reached his front yard, where her SUV was parked, he said, "I'd really like to help her, too. I've tried. But the FBI is on my back, and now that U.S. Marshal. I'm worried anything we do to get in touch with her might only call attention to her. It's better if we all lay low and wait."

She nodded. "Yeah. I guess she can handle herself."

"But if she does get in touch, I'll be sure to let her know I spoke to you," he added.

She smiled. "Thanks. Tell her . . ." She thought for a moment. "Tell her that she has more allies than she knows. That we all believe her, and want to see her come home."

"Will do." He watched her get into her car, and with a wave, she drove away.

Yes, it was hard for all of them, especially her family. He wished there was something he could do to prove her innocence. But there were no easy answers. Right now, until Kane Wilcox stopped tightening the noose, he'd have to keep cool and bide his time. Unfortunately, that was all any of them could do.

CHAPTER THIRTEEN

There were no cars on the way back to Brackettville. Not a single one.

Mia had to walk the whole way back, seven miles, in heat that was well over 115 degrees. The sun drifted high into the sky, painting everything a bright white. Without sunglasses, Mia felt like her eyeballs were about to explode with pain. Her head pounded and the sun scalded her shoulders. Ahead of her, the horizon blurred, miles and miles of straight, gently rolling hills, into a hazy oblivion. Vultures cawed above, eagerly waiting to make her their next meal.

Not today, boys, she thought, struggling to put one foot in front of the other.

She drained her water bottle fully during the walk, and by the time she stumbled in past the city limits, her clothes were drenched in sweat.

She threw open the door to the motel's office and took a moment to relish the glorious air pouring through the central air conditioning. It felt like heaven.

"Forty dollars. Just leave it on the counter," Sue's voice croaked. "You can have number—"

"It's me," Mia said, panting.

"Oh, you," Sue said. She was obviously still sore over Mia finding and dismantling her spy-cam in room twelve. "Check-out's at noon. If you plan on staying another night, you need to pay in advance."

Mia checked the clock on the wall. "I'm not sure I am," she said, going to the brochure rack and staring at it. She rummaged through a few of the stacks, throwing clouds of dust everywhere, until she found what she was looking for. It was an old brochure that might have been done in the sixties, considering the dated font and the picture of the family on the front. The mother had a beehive, and the father was wearing plaid Bermuda shorts, and they were smiling as if they'd just won the lottery.

The brochure said: *RISING SUN CAMPGROUND! A place to get away from it all.*

Free pool! Restaurant on site! Close to Major Attractions!

Your Oasis in the beautiful and friendly Chihuahuan Desert! Come visit us!

She flipped through it, looking for some kind of map, and found one, but none of the roads seemed to mean anything to her.

Mia brought the brochure over to the counter and held it out to Sue, who was still seated on the couch, a bowl of something that looked like Spaghettios resting on her chest. She glanced over at it. "That place has been closed forever."

"Okay, but it's not officially closed. Your son told me that."

She startled as if Mia had just announced that aliens had landed outside. Pulling the bowl off her chest, she struggled to her feet and waddled over to the desk. "You saw him? You saw my Davey?"

"I saw the man named Coop. Is he your son?"

She nodded. "David Cooper. He's my boy. How did he look?"

"Fine. I guess." He looked like a man who'd spent far too long, living in the desert, without running water and the little luxuries of everyday life. "But I'm sorry, I don't think I'll be able to talk sense into him. He seems pretty happy up there, selling drugs to a bunch of transients."

She leaned over the counter, breathing hard. "I know. I know he's a good boy, though. What a shame. He was such a good boy. Went to college. He's just on the wrong path, ever since he came back. I just don't know what to do with him."

"Anyway," Mia said, pointing at the brochure. "Do you know anything about what happened to this place after the campground closed down?"

She squinted at it. "Yeah. It's not a campground anymore. More like a commune. Some big-time movie executive retired from the business in LA, tired of the rat-race, and moved out here to start some kind of utopian community for other people like him. I hear he has about a hundred people living up there with him."

"A movie exec? Really?"

"Oh, yeah. His name was Brunley. Brent Brunley. I looked him up on IMDB when I first heard about it. He's responsible for some big-budget, superhero-type movies. David was into them. I never was. But anyway, he and his wife moved out here and started the community. They live off the grid, from what I hear. They don't make trouble, so no one troubles them."

Mia nodded. "Do you happen to know where it is? This map isn't really--"

She grabbed it and studied it closely. "Yes. The Old Mesquite Trail used to be a road, but when the tourism dried up around here, and the hotel closed, no one used it anymore. It's nothing but dirt now, heading out into the mountains. But I'd say it's a good ten miles there. Can you walk that on foot?"

Every part of her body seemed to revolt at the thought. She was so tired. But she really didn't have any other choice. "I walked seven miles on the highway, back from the Alamo Village, so I guess."

"Bless you," she said, shuddering. "I can't do much walking anymore. Hurts my trick knee. If you do go, you'd better go pretty quick. You don't want to get caught out there at night, without supplies, at least."

"I've got supplies," she said, holding up her bag, though they were pretty meager. "Can I fill up my water bottle here before I go?"

Sue's lips twisted. "I suppose. I guess that means you ain't staying another night?"

She shook her head. She couldn't walk twenty miles in a single day. She'd probably wind up camping in the desert. Though camping had never been her favorite thing, she'd grown pretty used to it, since her escape. Sleeping out under the stars wasn't the worst thing, not when you'd slept in a tiny prison cell, thinking that would be your home for the rest of your life.

"Then it'll be two bucks to fill that up," she said, pointing to her water bottle.

"Two bucks? Seriously?"

Sue nodded, entirely serious. "You clean everything out of your room?"

"Yes." Mia gave it over. It would probably be tap water, and have that awful, metallic taste like the water in her hotel room, but she didn't have time to argue. She needed to get on the road. She stooped down and adjusted her socks, making sure she didn't have blisters, and when she stood up, Sue was there with her full bottle of water. As expected, it had a bit of a yellow tinge to it. But it was better than nothing.

Mia pulled two dollars out of her change purse and grabbed the water. "Thanks for this."

Sue watched her, her pudgy hands on her hips. "What do you think you're going to find out there, girl? News about this Loring girl? What's it all matter to you?"

"I told you. I'm a friend of the family," she said. "That's all."

She made a clucking sound with her tongue. "Hmm. Sounds like an awful lot of trouble to go through for family. You walk ten miles out there, you gotta walk ten miles back. You'd better take another bottle of water for that. This one, on the house. I don't want your death on my hands." She smacked a bottle down. "If you ask me, it's silly. The police haven't figured anything out. What makes you think you will?"

"I don't know, but all I know is that I have to do something. If something happened to your son, wouldn't you want to know who did it and why?"

Sue stared at her for a long time, then nodded. "I guess so." She pocketed the two dollars in the front pocket of her housedress and said, "I can't promise your room will still be here when you get back, you know. We do sometimes get busy on weekends."

Mia nodded, thanked the woman, and left. She hoped that she'd never have to come back, and that the Rising Sun brought her the answers the was looking for.

CHAPTER FOURTEEN

Why did I think I could walk this?

Mia glanced behind her. The town of Bracketville was still visible in the distance, and yet she was already tired, her feet aching. The sun seemed even hotter than it had been at midday. Flies swarmed her, feasting on what was exposed of her sweaty skin. Not much of it was exposed because she wore a loose jacket over her head to protect from sunburn, but it didn't seem to help. It was like the sun was burning through her layers of clothing.

She kept staring at her feet, placing one foot in front of the other as she walked the rough terrain. It was mostly flat, but there were small rocks and bushes in the way, and of course, she had to keep alert for rattlesnakes.

But it was all the same, for miles and miles. No change to the dusty, barren landscape. As she trudged along the narrow path, thoughts kept intruding.

Soon, she found herself remembering that time that her whole family had gone camping to Big Bend National Park, south of Dallas. Kelsey had just been a toddler. She'd never been camping before, but it had been such a long time since they'd gone on a vacation, she didn't care. Aidan had been so excited, since he was the outdoorsy type, so he'd planned all these activities he'd hoped to do. He'd imagined forging trails and going paddling on the river, all with Kelsey wrapped up like a burrito in a little baby carrier, on his back.

But of course, it hadn't worked out that way. They were ill-equipped to go on any outing, much less a camping trip, with a baby in tow. Kelsey had cried the whole time, and they'd barely walked half a mile with her before she started to wail. She was up every night, crying . . .

They wound up cutting the camping trip, their first vacation in years, short. It was just another reminder that post-kids, everything would be different. She remembered wondering if they'd ever be able to get away on vacation, again.

Funny how back then, that had seemed like a major problem. How the thought of all those years of raising Kelsey had seemed like they'd go on for a lifetime.

Now, they were slipping through her fingers, and she wished desperately that she could put them on pause.

She looked up again, and it seemed cooler, as the sun was now settling beyond the milk-chocolate mountains in the distance. After that, the temperatures felt more comfortable. She was able to walk and actually enjoy the sights and scenery. The desert wasn't dead—it was very much alive with all kinds of creatures and interesting flora. She'd grabbed a branch from an old mesquite tree and used that as a walking stick.

It was shortly after that that she began to see the signs—huge billboards, some missing planks, most so faded that they were almost nothing but a sea of white. Some had been reduced to just a couple of poles, dug into the hard earth. She finally managed to see one—*WELCOME TO PEACE AND RELAXATION OF THE RISING SUN CAMPGROUND! 2 MILES STRAIGHT AHEAD!* with a picture of a typical oasis, with palm trees and water.

If it weren't for them, she'd probably have thought she was on the wrong path. It looked like there was nothing ahead of her, and when she turned to see how far she had come, nothing behind her. Like she was the only person alive on Earth. But that sign made her steps surer, until she came upon another one. The other signs, she could only make out the words RISING SUN, so her heart thudded with anticipation.

When she passed the last sign, she finally saw something other than the desert up ahead. It looked like a thin, chain-link fence. She picked up her pace and stopped in front of the gate, where another sign was far less welcoming than the others leading up to it.

RISING SUN CAMPGROUND CLOSED

NO TRESPASSING

She laced her fingers between the fence openings and stared through it at what was beyond. There were several small buildings, made entirely of recycled materials—planks of mismatched, painted woods, rusted, corrugated metal, and scraps of whatever else had been lying around. There were a few other outbuildings that looked to be in better condition, and one large building at the very back. A sign in faded script up above the door said, OFFICE. Other than that, she saw what looked like an outdoor firepit with boulders set around it, the kind scouts would tell stories around at night. A clothing line hung from one cabin to another, with several articles of white clothing, hanging from it, long-dry from the heat.

It seemed like it was deserted. There wasn't a single sign of life at all.

Mia looked down at the opening for the gate and realized it wasn't padlocked. In fact, all she had to do is lift the latch and step inside.

She hesitated for a moment, then pushed open the latch. The gate swung open, creaking slightly.

The moment the gate closed behind her, a tall man in overalls stepped out of the office building and spotted her. He strode over, a big smile on his face.

"I thought I heard someone out here!" he said as he approached. His face was tanned from the sun, his long hair a bleached blonde, so that he reminded Mia of a California surfer, minus the board. He was barefoot, the overalls hanging loose over his lean, athletic frame. "What can I help you with, ma'am?"

She hoisted her backpack onto her shoulder and said, "Is this Rising Sun, the commune?"

"It is, indeed," he said, his smile falling. "Are you looking for someone? Because if you are, I'll have to tell you that most people come here wanting to get away from everyone else. We're a family, here, and we protect our people. So we don't allow outsiders to visit."

"Actually," she said with a smile, "I want to get away. I heard about this place and I wanted to see what you were all about. Are you accepting new members?"

"Are we?" The smile was back. "We are! Of course! We are all about our family. Come on in. I'd love to show you around."

She smiled, relaxed, and accepted his hooked arm as he offered it to her. "I'm Paul, by the way."

"Danielle," she said, saying the first name that sprang to her mind.

He walked her deeper into the compound and said, "You've caught us at a quiet time, Danielle. We were all in our leader's quarters, having our daily meeting." He squinted toward the office, where a number of individuals began to pour out of the doors. Mia noticed most of the women were wearing white tunic dresses, and the men were wearing overalls without shirts underneath. They were all similarly tanned and thin. "Ah, looks like it's over. Come on, I'll show you around."

He led her down the middle of what was the main road in the commune, waving to people as he went. All of them smiled back at him, and some said, "Hi, Brother Paul."

People smiled and nodded at her. They all seemed so content, so peaceful. She found herself smiling back, forgetting the pain in her feet as she followed, eager to find out more about the place.

Mia noticed a small garden, with a bunch of people working it, pulling out the biggest, ripest tomatoes she'd ever seen. "This is where we get most of our food," he explained, grabbing a few cherry tomatoes from a vine. "Try one. You'll never have better."

She took one and popped it into her mouth. He was right. She'd never had a tomato that was so sweet and flavorful. "Wow, how do you get the water in order to—"

"The compound is fed by a spring from the Rio Grande. We never have to worry about water around here, or food, for that matter. We have plenty to go around," he said, popping a tomato in his mouth as he led her to the next tent, the one with the line of clothing hanging outside. Inside, a couple women were washing clothes. "This is the wash-house. Hello, Sisters Holly and Barbie!"

"Hello, Brother Paul!" they called back in unison. They were both busy scrubbing clothes on an old washboard, which looked like hard work, and yet, Mia had never seen any people so thrilled to be doing the laundry.

He waved at them, closed the flap on the tent, and said, "We all have jobs in this commune. No one is more important than anyone else. We give it our all, and we expect the same in return."

"What's your job?" she asked him.

Paul laughed. "Other than being the town welcome wagon and tour-giver? I also manage our leader's day-to-day affairs. I guess you could call me the second in command."

"Who is your leader?"

"Brother Brent. He's a good man. One of the best. We all love him here. He's very giving and wise," Paul said, leading her down another aisle. He opened a door to another tent, full of piles of canned goods and toiletries. "This, here, is our store, where you can pick up any necessities you might need. It's all free, of course. Money is of no use to us, here."

A few children ran past them, in little more than tunics and underpants, playing with a red ball and squealing with excitement.

"Hello, Brother Paul!" the oldest boy, who must've been around twelve, shouted.

Paul ruffled the kid's shaggy hair and watched him kick the ball into a makeshift goal. "Hey, little one. Nice shot!" He strolled a little farther and pointed. "Over there is our school. We teach the kids reading and writing and arithmetic, of course, but also the life skills they need to grow into an adult. Farming, cooking, hunting, socializing, taking care of their home . . . things like that."

Mia nodded. "Sounds great."

"It really is. We have something special here." He opened another tent flap to a series of long tables. "Our mess hall. We love nothing more than to share meals and fellowship together, so our mealtimes are sacred, and observed regularly at six in the morning, noon, and six in the evening."

"Is it religious?"

"No, we welcome all religions. There is a certain reverence, though, toward Mother Nature, who sustains us, and gives us so many of our blessings."

"Ah. So about your founder . . . Brent Brunley, right? I read about him, which was what made me curious. He's a former movie producer who wanted a simpler life?"

He stopped walking and smiled benevolently down at her. "He's Brother Brent, here. Our people shed their last names when they come to us. They leave all the trappings of their previous, more complicated lives behind, to enjoy a simple, more peaceful existence. So as far as what Brother Brent did in another lifetime? It's of no importance to any of us. All that matters is the now."

"Oh, I see," she said, feeling sufficiently scolded. "So . . . if I wanted to join, what would I have to do?"

He laughed. "We're pretty informal here. There isn't much of an application process. Just say you want in, and you're in."

"Really? But—"

"Like I said, people come here for a variety of reasons, but the one thing we have in common is wanting a better life for ourselves. One-hundred percent of the time, people find that here. We don't advertise, and yet, we are always admitting new family members. We've doubled our numbers in just the last two years. Our community is growing because we're so special. People appreciate that and want the best for all of us, as a whole. It's that family connection that makes us special."

"But what if someone doesn't fit in?"

Paul pointed at the gate. "Our gates aren't guarded. We understand that everyone's different. People may leave at any time. But no one ever has. Why should they, when they find paradise?" He winked.

Paradise? So, either he was lying, or Rachel was never here. It sounded so good, though, Mia found herself wondering . . . if the police really left this place alone, could she hide out here indefinitely? The thought danced in her head, but quickly danced out. She had Kelsey and Aiden. She couldn't leave them behind.

Plus, places like this were often too good to be true. She still doubted it. Especially knowing about the death of those women. "Goodness. Isn't there anything bad about this place?"

He laughed some more. "Ah, you caught me. I'm a good salesman for this place, because I love it so much, but there are definitely some things that people might not like. First of all, we're dry here. No alcohol or drugs permitted. Secondly, we don't allow any outside visitors, or really, anything from the outside, to intrude. Either you're a member of our family, or you're not. We find when people socialize with the world at large, they tend to bring its problems with them. All the news of the outside world—its wars, its illness, its violence—we leave that behind. And we prefer to make a clean break, which means we're happier."

She had to admit, she liked that idea. She always used to be too glued to her phone and the 24/7 news, and often, it would all put her in a bad mood. "That sounds nice."

Paul gave her two thumbs up. "So, you're interested?"

She nodded. Even if it didn't sound amazing, she wanted to stay. She felt like she was close to something. She could just imagine those other women, coming out here, eager to be a part of this family. It was a little odd, yes, but dazzling, how happy everyone seemed.

"Let me tour you around a little more. Over here, we have our lodging tents and cabins," he said, opening the door to one. "This one here is mine. It's not much, but I find I don't have a need for much. We really give up all our worldly goods when we stay here, for the good of the people."

"All of them? So I'd be expected to surrender my—"

"You're not *expected* to. But most people do. Once they realize that everything we have is theirs, they tend to willingly give up their things. They realize that there is better use for them when shared."

“Oh.” She peeked inside. He was right. It was just a small bed, a dresser. That was it. Nothing personal. “Does everyone get their own room?”

“Not everyone. I have to admit we’re having a few growing pains, so until we build the new cabins, some of the newer arrivals have had to team up and bunk together. But it’s good. Like those old days in college. Besides, we don’t spend much time in our rooms. We all work, have meals together, and in the evenings, there are a lot of opportunities for fellowship. We have dances, and a number of clubs you can be involved in, according to your interests. Bridge club is always very popular, and our flag football games are exciting. Do you like bridge?”

“Never played, actually.”

“Well, we’ll be sure to teach you, and soon, you’ll be winning with the best of us.” He motioned to the big office. “Would you like to meet Brother Brent, now? He’s always keen to meet our newest family members first, to welcome them to the fold.”

“Sure,” she said, following him up the stairs to the main building in the compound. As she did, she looked around at the group of people, all engaged in their various duties for the good of the community. She had to admit, to someone who didn’t have a place in the world, it probably looked like heaven.

So had Rachel been here? Either she hadn’t, or someone here wasn’t telling the truth, and Mia was determined to find out which it was.

CHAPTER FIFTEEN

For some reason, Mia's palms were slick with sweat as she was led into the main office to meet with Brent Brunley. Or, Brother Brent, as he was known among the members of Rising Sun.

It was probably because, despite the rather simple look of the other accommodations, the office was clearly much nicer, from the moment she stepped inside. That was because an air conditioner was purring gently in the window, making the home feel much more comfortable than outside.

But it wasn't just that. The place smelled lightly of citrus, and the main room was decorated with rich brocade wallpaper and shining brass fixtures. The floors were a dark but glimmering hardwood. There was a reception desk, but no one was sitting there. Off to the right was what had to have been the meeting room, with a number of long benches. At the left, though, behind double French doors, was a room with elegant furnishings, velvet-covered couches and soft, thick carpeting.

She had to admit, it reminded her a little bit of *Animal Farm,* where the pigs started living in the farmhouse and nobody could tell the difference between them and the humans anymore. The whole, "We're all equal, but some of us are more equal than others!" thing. But though it was setting off mild alarm bells in her head, she kept along with it. This was the introductory phase, where everything was roses and sunshine. If there was a bait-and-switch, she'd have to hold out and become a full-fledged member of the family.

I can do this, she thought to herself, her face flushing even with the air conditioning's pleasantly cool air blowing on her skin. *Just keep calm and be agreeable.*

Brother Paul said, "Wait here," and stepped through the doors, disappearing out of sight.

She wandered around and noticed a photograph on the wall. It said: *Rising Sun First Family.* The photograph showed about two dozen smiling, tanned faces, standing on the porch of the office, holding shovels and hoes.

"That was when we first moved out here, twenty years ago," a voice said behind her.

She turned to see a man standing next to Brother Paul who could've been his twin. Older, probably in his late fifties, he was just as tall, blonde, and tan, but he was dressed more professionally, in a loose button-down shirt and slacks. But his blue eyes were much more intense. Mia couldn't help but feel unnerved.

He fixed her with a smile and said, "Brother Paul says you're interested in joining our family. I am Brother Brent." He extended his hand to her.

She shook his hand, noting how cold his fingertips felt in hers. "I am Danielle."

"Sister Danielle. I'm so pleased to meet you. Why don't you join me and Paul? We were just about to have lunch."

"All right."

She expected him to lead her outside to the mess hall, but instead, they went in the opposite direction, deeper into the house. She found herself in an elegant dining room, with a massive oak dining table and high-backed chairs. The table could've held twenty people, but it was set for just three.

Odd. How had he known she'd be here? The back of her neck prickled. "It's almost like you were expecting me," she remarked.

Brent tittered and took his place at the head of the table. "We've been getting new family members in almost every day, lately. It's lovely to see how our community is thriving, from the twenty-three individuals I brought with me to start this project, two decades ago."

She sat down. "How many residents do you have now?"

"Over one-hundred and fif—" Paul began, Brent shot him a look—not necessarily a reproachful or angry look, but it made Paul stop, mid-sentence.

"One-sixty-three," Brent said proudly, lacing his hands in front of him on the table. "And it is my responsibility, as leader here, to care for each of them. I'm like a proud daddy, and each resident here is one of my babies."

The back door opened, and a woman in a tunic appeared. Brent made some kind of hand-signal to her, and she nodded and quickly disappeared from where she'd come.

"You see," he said, leaning back and smiling. "When I envisioned my little slice of heaven, I imagined a place far removed from the anxieties and frustrations of everyday life. I'm ashamed to say it now, but I lived a very high-profile, high-pressure life, and it was exhausting. I wanted to get back to the olden days, the days when you put in an honest day's work to put food on the table, make sure the family was provided for, and that's it. The simple life. And I can tell many others wanted the same, considering how fast we've been growing."

"It sounds very nice," she said, as the door opened once again and the woman appeared, rolling a cart with three silver-lidded dishes on it. She placed one in front of each of the diners, very carefully, hardly making a sound.

Brent lifted his lid first and stared at the food, his lip curling slightly in disgust. "Pepper sauce, Frances," he said with a wide smile. "How many times do I have to tell you that I can't eat steak au poivre without extra pepper sauce?"

The woman let out a little squeak and rushed to his side with the gravy boat. She tipped some more onto his meat, until he sliced his hand through the air to stop her.

"Offer some to our guest," he instructed.

She started to, but Mia said, "I'm good."

He sliced off a piece, stabbed it with his fork, and popped it in his mouth, then closed his eyes. "You really should try it with the extra peppercorn sauce. It's incredible."

"I'm sorry . . ." she said, a little confused. "I didn't see any livestock out there. Did I miss it, or did—"

"No, you did not. We try to be as self-sufficient as possible, but with some things, such as meat, it's more economical for us to trade with other communities. So we trade vegetables with a local rancher for the best beef you'll ever taste," he explained, chewing. "Paul, here, is in charge of making those arrangements. But we like to keep as closed off from regular society as possible. I'm sure Paul told you?"

She nodded. "That's probably a good thing. Things are pretty crazy outside your gates."

"Trust me, I know. I'm a bit of a mother hen to my people. I want to protect them from all that. And so far, I really have."

Mia looked up and noticed a giant painting of Brent, on the wall. In it, he looked handsome, dignified, and benevolent and had a bit of a golden aura around his head.

He must've caught her looking because he said, "My family made that for me for my fiftieth birthday, last year. They're talented, are they not?"

"It's very nice," she said, though she had to admit, it was a little creepy. It seemed to be watching her.

"So, Danielle," he said, finishing his steak. "Tell us. What brings you here? Why do you want to join our family?"

She glanced uncomfortably at Paul. "I thought that didn't matter—"

"It doesn't. Not to anyone out there." He pointed toward the front of the cabin. "But like I said, I'm in charge of these people's safety, and I want to make sure you'll fit with us. I'm sure you'll understand, but we can't have just anyone infiltrating our borders."

That wasn't what Paul had said, but she understood it. But maybe it was a recent change of policy. Maybe it was as a result of something that had happened in the past. Perhaps with Rachel . .

"I understand. It's not a problem," she said with a smile. The slight hesitation had given her time to concoct a story, since there was no way she was going to tell them the truth. "I was living upstate, working a boring nine-to-five desk job, and I got so burned out. I was on a message board, talking with people who had made really big changes in their lives, and one of them mentioned communes, and how they work off-the-grid and really help people concentrate on what's important. So I asked around, and someone mentioned that they had a brother who went here. So, I thought I'd check it out. And here I am."

"Yes, here you are," he said. "That's a familiar story. We get many people who are fed up with the rat race, don't we, Paul?"

Paul nodded. "So many. It's not unusual in these days."

"Before you can join us, though," Brent said, "You should fully understand the rules that you'll be expected to comply with. I believe Paul might have told you some of what you could expect?"

Mia nodded. "Yes. That I'm not allowed to interact with the outside world, and how I'll be expected to surrender my things and work as part of the family?"

"That's right. One: We'll take your things, and hold them in safekeeping in the event you should want to leave. Two: After you submit to a search, we'll give you your standard clothing—we have a dress code here, for modesty, so you'll be expected to dress in the provided garments. Three: You'll get your living quarters, and be given your job and trained on how to perform it to our satisfaction. That's about it. We try to keep things simple."

"You mentioned a search?"

"Yes. We have to do that, unfortunately. Too many travelers have attempted to bring weapons into our community, and we're peaceful. Weapons are not permitted."

That made sense, but it also meant that she'd have to part with the gun she'd taken from Wilson Andrews's lackey. Probably a good thing to get rid of it, anyway, since it wasn't hers to begin with. She mentally went through her possessions, making sure she had nothing else that would give her cover away. No . . . she didn't have any ID, any papers with her name on it. It would be okay.

"Oh . . . but I should tell you, I do have a gun."

They both looked at her. "Now, why is that, Danielle?" Brent asked kindly.

She shrugged. "It gets a little scary, backpacking alone, at night, as a woman. It's for safety."

"That's fine," Brent said with a smile. "I'm glad you told us. You'll have to surrender it, but don't worry. Your family is all the protection you need."

"That's fine with me."

He motioned to her food. "Something wrong with your meal?"

"Oh, no. It's delicious. I'm just a little excited to be a part of this. It sounds so great," she gushed, hoping she wasn't overdoing it. "My stomach's doing flip-flops."

"All right, then, let's not waste any time, shall we?" he said brightly, pushing away from the chair. The woman appeared, and he snapped his fingers at her. She bowed slightly to him and followed.

That is so bizarre, she thought.

He led her to a long hallway, then stopped in front of a door. "Give me your bag, now. I'll take care of the items inside. You go in here and Lina will perform the search and give you something to change into. For your privacy, of course."

She hesitated. The last thing she wanted to do was submit to that invasion of privacy, but if she wanted to find out what was happening, she had to play by their rules.

"Thank you," she said, stepping inside a room that looked like a medical exam room. There was a long table in the center of it, a sink, and various cabinets. It was white and clinical.

Lina was still bowing, hunched over, when they were alone. She said, in a mouse-quiet voice, "If you turn around, spread your legs slightly and raise your arms, I'll only take a second. I know it's weird."

"It's fine," she said, complying.

The girl's hands patted her down thoroughly. It clearly wasn't the woman's first frisk. She ran her hands down Mia's sides, up between her legs, carefully checking her. Mia also noticed she did a fair amount of checking her rib cage, looking for a wire. Though Coop had said they flew under the local police's radar, there was clearly some distrust of law enforcement there.

After several minutes of searching, Lina opened one of the cabinets and pulled out one of the simple, white linen shifts. "Here you go," she said quietly. "You can wear this."

"What about shoes . . . underwear?" Mia asked, feeling silly.

Lina shook her head. "Brother Brent says its best to stay as simple as possible."

"But he was wearing—"

"Yes, well, he interacts with other people in order to get us supplies. So he has to present a more professional front," she said, looking down at her bare, dirty feet. "It's a lot easier to get dressed in the morning, anyway."

Mia shook out the tunic. It was thin and would barely reach her lower thigh. There was so much wrong with this, but she pushed it aside. "Thank you."

"I'll wait outside," she said, gnawing on her dry lip.

"Wait. Lina," she said, wanting to ask her more. For the dirt, the nitty-gritty that wasn't on the official tour. "Do you really like it here?"

She blinked, then nodded.

"If you could do it again, would you?"

"Yes. The Rising Sun is my life."

Mia smiled at her. "So it's pretty great? Where did you come from, before this?"

She glanced toward the door. "We're not—we're really not supposed to talk about our lives before."

"I'm sure it's okay. Brent asked me—"

"He can ask you at the initial meeting. But after that, he better not catch you talking about it, again. You'll—" She sucked in a breath, and Mia filled in what she imagined Lina was going to say. *You'll be punished.* "He just doesn't like that. He likes his people to stay in the here and now. That's all."

"But he's a good man, isn't he? Fair and –"

"Oh, yes. Brother Brent is the best man. I—" Her eyes got a bit faraway and dreamy. "Everyone thinks so. He's so handsome. So strong. So capable . . ."

That sounded a little odd. Mia wanted to ask more, but Lina backed herself against the door, scrambling for the knob.

"I've taken too long. I've got to go," she whispered, and slipped outside.

When Lina was gone, Mia looked around the room. She started to pace, thinking. That woman, Lina, was clearly terrified. Of what? If this was where Rachel and the others had gone and met their ends, then a massive cover-up was underway. And she just needed to ride it out, see where it led.

As she was pacing, she looked into the corner of the room and noticed something, very small, just a little black dot on the wall.

A camera. They were watching her.

She quickly changed out of her clothes and pulled the tunic on, then went out to the hallway. The two men were standing there, waiting for her.

"Great. That looks wonderful, Sister Danielle," Brent said, taking her hand. "We're so happy to welcome you to our family. Let's get you introduced to a few of the people you'll be working with and show you where you'll be staying."

He strode out onto the porch of the main office and paused there, taking a deep gulp of the stagnant, oppressively hot air as he scanned the workings of his community. Everyone seemed to be scrambling about like worker bees. He nodded in approval, motioned to them, and she and Paul followed.

"Now, Sister Danielle," he said in a calm and pleasant tone. "We're growing, and constant growing means we need more help with just about everything. So I thought I'd give you a choice. Would you like to work in the garden, or would you be interested in the laundry?"

She pointed to her red nose. "Do you have any sunblock?"

"We do, but that looks pretty nasty. Is that starting to blister? We'll get you first aid for that immediately," he said, eyeing her closely. Then he clapped his hands together. "All right, I think it's settled, then. You'll work the laundry with Holly and Barbie. That'll be perfect, because you'll be sharing a bunk-house with them. They're the two live wires of the place, I'll tell you. Let's go."

"Um . . . sharing a bunk house?" she asked.

"Yes—we're making plans to give everyone their own house, but we keep growing, and so . . .," he shrugged. "What can you do? Growing pains."

They walked across the dusty field toward the wash-house. The dirt felt strange and hot under Mia's bare feet, and several times, she winced after stepping on a small stone. She'd never liked going barefoot. Finally, he pulled back the tent flaps and let Mia go through.

"Girls, girls!" he said with great excitement. "I have news for you!"

"Hello, Brother Brent!" one said, as if a rock star had just graced them with his presence. The other said, "Oh, thank you for visiting!"

"You may have met her before," he said, presenting Mia to them. One of them was tall and statuesque, with model-like looks, and the other was short, a bit older, and a little rounder. They both had their dark hair pulled into ponytails, with no make-up. "But this is the lovely Sister Danielle. Sister Danielle, may I present the gorgeous Sister Holly and the delightful Sister Barbie."

They both giggled. "Hi, Sister Danielle," Barbie said in a high-pitched squeak of a voice. "It's nice to meet you, and even nicer knowing you're going to be helping us with all this laundry!"

They all laughed hysterically. Mia smiled along with it, though she couldn't think of anything she'd like to do less than laundry. She said, "I'm happy to help."

"Don't worry, though," Brother Brent said, squeezing her shoulder. "We'll give you some time to get comfortable first, and then we'll start you with light duty. We don't want to scare you off!"

They all smiled and laughed and talked some more, and it all seemed very cordial, like all was perfectly well. But there was something going on, an undercurrent of tension flowing through the tent. She'd been in the FBI for a long time. She knew fake smiles when she saw them, and now she needed to find out exactly what they were hiding.

CHAPTER SIXTEEN

The steam in the wash-tent was almost unbearable. But Mia noticed that the two women, Holly and Barbie, didn't seem to mind it at all. They worked cheerfully, telling stories about their time at Rising Sun.

Barbie, the older one, who was probably in her late fifties, said that she was one of the original members of the commune. She didn't say anything about her old life, before Rising Sun, but she continually gushed about Brother Brent, and how he single-handedly put in motion the events that led to the building of this grand community. Holly, too, waxed poetic about their esteemed leader, but concentrated on their future plans.

"We're not always going to wash clothes this way," she said with a smile, sweat or water from the steam running down her temples as she scrubbed away on the washboard. "Brother Brent says that we'll be constructing towers to harness the power of the wind and the sun, and then we'll be able to use that energy to operate actual washing machines. So I think in the next years, our job will become easier."

Barbie wagged a finger at her. "Not that we want to slack off."

"Oh, no! I just think that if we had that, we'd have more time to do other things. There's always so much to do around here. I'd love to plant flowers around Brother Brent's house. He says he loves them."

Barbie nodded. "That would be nice. Maybe we could do it as a surprise for him? The Sun Feast is coming up."

"Oh!" Holly clapped her hands. "We should! I love the Sun Feast. Is the planning for the event already underway?"

"Sun Feast?" Mia asked.

Barbie nodded and leaned into Mia. "You'll learn, Sister Danielle, to love the Sun Feast. It's the day we all come together to celebrate our love for our fellow man. It's really something special. And it's happening in a couple weeks."

Holly said, "It's also Brother Brent's birthday!"

Mia watched the two of them scrub, wondering if she should offer to help. Holly's fingers were red and raw. "What happened to your hands?"

She laughed. "Oh, I just get a little over-excited with the scrubbing. Like Brother Brent says, cleanliness is the hallmark of a Rising Sun. We're supposed to wash up at least five times a day, in the morning, before meals, and at night. It gets very dirty with all the dust here, as you might have noticed. So we have to stay clean!"

Mia looked down at her feet. They were already dirty due to the walk from the office to the wash tent. "That must be really hard."

"You'll get used to it," Barbie assured her, struggling to lift a basket full of clothes.

"Let me get that!" Mia called, rushing to her side.

"Oh, no," Barbie said, swatting her off. "Like Brother Brent said, you should relax for now. You'll have plenty of time to get involved, later. But I appreciate it, Sister Danielle."

They worked and worked until the sun had gone down. So much of the wash had been cleaned and folded, and yet there were still piles and piles to get to. Suddenly, a whistle sounded.

Barbie yawned. "Oh, there it is," she said, untying her apron.

"What is that?" Mia asked, pulling herself off the stool she'd perched on.

"It's time for our evening meal."

Holly stopped what she was doing and wiped her face with the bib of her apron. She slipped it off and said, "I guess this will just have to wait!"

"Until tomorrow?" Mia asked, following her out of the tent.

"No . . . until tonight. We have to finish up with all the laundry before we go to bed," Barbie said. "It's the rules. We don't put off until tomorrow what should be done today."

"Oh . . . and you start in the morning? That's a long day."

"It can be, at first," Barbie said as they stepped out into the night. It was already chilly, and Mia hugged herself. "But you will get used to it. I can tell you, there is nothing like putting a good, honest day of work in. Sore in the bones, sane in the head, is what Brother Brent always says. And he's right."

Mia noticed the flood of people, all headed into the dining tent. They fell in line. In the tent, every table was crowded with people. As she stood in line to get her food, she noticed that the men and women were separated, the men closer to the buffet line, the women toward the back. Holly handed her a plate, and she held it out for the server, who dropped a scoop of what looked like rice in some red sauce, onto her plate, and a piece of white bread.

It was nothing like the meal she'd been served in the office, that was for sure. Mia stared at it, wondering if that was all they were going to get. When she looked back at the men, they each had a couple of drumsticks. But when they reached the end of the line and took their utensils, all she had was the tiny helping of rice, spreading over the plate.

"Is this all we get?" Mia asked Holly. At that moment, she was too uneasy to be hungry, but she was curious.

"Oh, yes. They run out of the meat pretty quickly, so if you're not first in line, you're out of luck. Growing pains," she said with a shrug. "But I'm a vegetarian, so I don't mind."

They each grabbed a cup of tepid water and turned toward the tables, balancing their food. Barbie led them to the back of the tent, where Mia squeezed onto a bench with a number of other women.

"Everyone! This is Sister Danielle!" Barbie said as she sat. "She's going to be helping us in the laundry, and bunking in our room!"

The women all smiled, and one of them clapped slightly, and another said, "Oh, wonderful!" They introduced themselves, though their names quickly went out of her head. Most of them were older, but a couple were young, probably in their early twenties. Maybe they knew Rachel.

She unrolled her napkin with her utensils, trying to think of how to broach the subject.

But she couldn't find a good way to do it. They all seemed famished, digging into their food without conversation. Mia took a forkful of her rice and tasted it. It was bland; it needed salt. Forgetting the food in front of her, she looked around at the people. They were all very ordinary, except for their clothes. The men wore overalls, and then women, those tiny tunics. She noticed a couple of men, eyeing the women, but that happened in regular society, too. Nothing seemed too out of sorts—it was just a bunch of women, eating after a hard day's work.

"Are you not going to eat that?" an elderly woman said to her, from across the table. She had pure white hair that had thinned so much that she could see her waxy scalp, and bright blue eyes.

She was pointing at Mia's bread. Mia said, "No, would you like it?"

The woman's eyes widened and she reached for it.

"Charlie!" Barbie scolded from across the table. "You know you can't."

Charlie snatched her hand back and her eyes fell to her lap. "I know."

"Why not?" Mia said, confused. "I'm not really hungry. I'm not going to eat it."

"If you're not going to eat it, you shouldn't have taken it," Barbie said, shaking her head. "You should eat it."

Okay, Mia thought, taking the bread in her hands. Now, everyone at the table was watching her. She took a bit of it. It was stale. *Happy?*

They seemed to be. Only Charlie was watching with longing, likely imagining the bread in her own stomach. Mia chewed slowly, swallowing the thick paste in her mouth, as the rest of the table cleared their plates and Holly banged the table.

"Everyone," she said, smiling. "I was just talking to Sister Barbie about Feast Day! It's not long from now and we were just thinking about planting flowers outside the office for Brother Brent!"

They all nodded, and one of them said, "Splendid idea."

Barbie said to the youngest one with the fiery red hair, "Sister June, since you work in the garden, can you see if Brother Ben will order us some flower seed?"

June clapped her hands. "Oh, we already have some! For the special project we were working on last year."

Barbie nodded. "Good, good. Do you want to spearhead this project?"

She patted her chest. "Me? It would be an honor!"

Mia felt like she'd entered the Twilight Zone. She was still a little freaked out over the whole bread incident. And now, they were all going crazy over planting flowers. Something was definitely off here. Yes, this was a simpler life, but it also felt weirdly restrictive, with new rules to follow that didn't seem to make much sense. She coughed, and a younger woman sitting next to Charlie, with a bush of dark hair and a long, pointed nose, looked at her.

"So tell us, Sister Danielle," she said in an accusing, rather dry voice. "What brings you here?"

"Just . . . looking to get away from the trials of everyday life," Mia explained, by now, very used to spouting that excuse.

"Hmm," the woman said, and Mia got the distinct impression that she didn't believe her. "You've come to the right place. But not everyone fits in here."

Holly gasped. "Oh, Sister Lola! Don't frighten her!" She turned to Mia and said, "Don't listen to that old negative Nelly. Most people do! We're all so friendly here."

"But if they don't . . .?" Mia asked, glad that Lola said it, because now she had something to work with. "They can just leave, right?"

"Of course! We don't put anyone in chains," Holly said with a laugh.

Lola snorted. "Some people, they've been more than happy to show the door. The troublemakers."

Wait, hadn't Brother Paul said that no one left this paradise? "Troublemakers?"

"There is trial period, of course. Thirty days to see if you like it," Barbie explained. "Sometimes after the first couple of days, people do decide it isn't for them, and that's fine. But no one has ever left after being fully initiated into our family."

Lola glared at her for a moment and said, "Yep, if anyone did, they'd get silenced real quick, if you disagree with anything the higher-ups say. You're expected to fall in line and—"

Barbie nudged her. "Oh, stop being so dramatic, Lola. We have rules, just like anyone. This isn't some totalitarian regime. Some people choose not to follow our way of life, and that's absolutely fine."

Lola said, "Sure it is," in a way that made Mia think she was being sarcastic.

This was the kind of thing Mia wanted to hear more of. "Oh?" she asked curiously. "What did they do?"

Lola opened her mouth to speak, but Barbie gave her a look that completely silenced the young woman, who started to push the remaining pieces of rice around her plate with her fork.

Barbie shook her head. "It might sound exciting, but I promise you, it's not all that juicy of gossip. Not everyone can adapt to our way of life. If people don't want to follow our rules, they're simply asked to leave. They collect their things, and we show them the door. That's all."

"Have many done that?" Mia asked. "Left after finding out what this place is all about?"

"A few have," Lola said. "And I haven't been here that long, but—"

"The vast majority of people stay," Barbie spoke over her, giving Lola a sidelong glance.

Mia had a feeling she'd never hear anything straight, as long as Barbie was around to talk over everyone and death-glare them into submission. She needed to take the bull by the horns.

"I heard about a girl that was found dead, not far from here? At Phantom Bridge?" she asked innocently, popping another piece of stale bread into her mouth. "Does anyone know anything about her? I was wondering if she was on her way here when she died, since it's so close."

That brought all conversation to a screeching halt. The women all exchanged glances, but none of them spoke.

That is, until Barbie said, "We try not to concern ourselves with outsider problems, but it doesn't surprise me. The desert can be a harsh place for someone who's alone. That's why we're so thankful for our oasis." She clapped her hands sharply again. "But it's too pleasant an occasion to speak of such terrible things. It puts a damper on everything! Let's talk more about the Sun Feast."

"Yes!" Holly said excitedly, and the others joined in, chattering about the plans for the event, that would involve food, dancing, music, and games. They sounded like PTA parents, planning their kids' holiday parties at school. The whole topic of the dead girl, found outside their gates, was quickly forgotten.

Mia, however, zoned out, thinking about Rachel Loring. The reports were that she had been headstrong. Had she come here, hoping to get away from it all, and then not fit in? Had she left? And then what?

By the time they finished their meals, the dining hall had cleared out. Another whistle blew, loud and long, startling Mia. "Do they always do that?" she asked, covering her ears.

Holly laughed. "You'll get used to it."

They walked outside, where Mia noticed a bunch of the men, gathered around a roaring fire, drinking from mugs. A few other men were engaged in what looked like a game of touch football. Holly and Barbie walked toward the wash-house, ignoring it all.

"So some people have to work, and some don't?" Mia asked, as the women all seemed to break and head in different directions.

"That's right. Some jobs are more work than others," Holly said. "Come on."

She hesitated. She knew that if she had to go in that stuffy tent to watch those women work the hours away, she'd be sick. And they hadn't even let her lift a hand yet. "I have to use the restroom," she said.

"Oh. The outhouses are over there," Holly said, pointing. "Do you want me to take you?"

Outhouses. Great. "No. I've got it. Thanks."

She headed that way, scanning the area as she walked. The men in the circle laughed loudly. She looked over at them and noticed a couple, staring at her. Skin crawling, she picked up the pace, noticing other things. Men, smoking cigarettes outside their tents. A couple playing checkers by moonlight. Talking in tight circles.

But no women. All of the women had scurried off to do work.

I'm probably overthinking this, she thought to herself. *I've only been here a few hours. I'm sure it's not that bad.*

She saw June walking up ahead and rushed to catch up to her. "Hi, uh, June?"

June looked over at her, but didn't stop. "Hey, there, Sister Danielle. How are you liking it here?"

She was walking at such a brisk pace, Mia had to shuffle into a slight run to keep up. "Well, it's different. What are you up to?"

"I have to work."

"Oh . . . I thought you worked in the garden. I figured at night—"

"Brother Ben likes the food storehouses to be tidied, to make sure that nothing is spoiled. I do that at night. And I'm late." She kicked into a run and took off.

Mia stopped walking. She looked around, feeling like a fish out of water. As she spun, she noticed a few other men, watching her. Their expressions weren't welcoming. They were more like . . . possessive. And they chilled Mia so much that a shiver ran down her spine.

She headed toward the outhouses. It was so dark there, she could barely see where she was going. As she passed a number of tents, a hand reached out and grabbed her.

She started to let out a yelp when she noticed the mass of gray, curly hair.

It was Charlie, the old lady from dinner, and her eyes were narrowed in a warning.

"What's wrong?" Mia asked. "Why are you—"

"You asked about that girl who was found dead in the desert. If we knew anything about it."

Mia nodded. "Do you?"

The woman gripped her wrist tightly, looked both ways to make sure the coast was clear, then whispered, "Yes. We all know her. Sister Rachel. She was here."

CHAPTER SEVENTEEN

"All right. That's the last basket of laundry. Time for bed."

Mia was snapped from her trance by that declaration. She'd been sitting on a stool in the corner for hours, waiting for the two busy bees to finish their jobs.

Meanwhile, she'd been thinking.

Rachel Loring had been here. She'd been living among them. It made sense that they wouldn't speak of it, considering her terrible fate, but were they responsible for it? Or had she left on her own and been killed afterwards? Whatever had happened, Mia now felt certain that the same thing had occurred to the other victims, Carrie Winters and Madison Lane.

She was getting closer. She could feel it.

Holly stretched her arms over her head as they prepared to leave the tent. "So how did you like your first day at Rising Sun?" she chirped.

"It was great," Mia said, now determined to play whatever part she needed to in order to keep suspicion off her. If the answers were here, the best thing she could do was fall in line and get people to trust her, let their guards down, so she could uncover the truth. "Do you work that long every day?"

"Oh, no. Today was just a hard one because the boys had a football tournament. They got extra dirty, so we had a lot of overalls to clean!" She giggled.

"So what do you do tomorrow morning?" Mia asked as she stepped out.

"Tomorrow, we'll start by delivering the clean clothes to every tent, and collecting the soiled garments to soak."

Barbie extinguished the lamp and joined them outside. By now, it was so frigid outside that she could see her breath in front of her. She'd experienced nights in the desert like this, where the temperature had dropped so significantly that it was a shock to the system, but she hadn't been wearing next-to-nothing.

She hugged herself, her teeth chattering. "Aren't you cold?"

"No," Barbie said, inhaling deeply through her nose. "I love this weather. It's so bracing! But there are plenty of blankets in our tent. You'll be nice and snug."

"Oh, dear," Holly said, putting a hand on her arm. "You're probably freezing because of that bad sunburn you got. Poor thing."

She nodded. "Brent mentioned something about first aid for the blisters on my nose?"

"No, I have something better for that in the tent," Barbie said. "Come on."

Mia had thought that since it was the three of them, and since Barbie had seniority, they'd take her to one of the larger tents. However, theirs was one of the smaller—a tiny, blue camping dome that they wouldn't even be able to stand in. When she and Aiden and Kelsey had gone to Big Bend, they'd had a bigger set-up.

"*This* is your tent?" she asked, shivering.

Barbie nodded, laughing. "It's all we need. Brings us closer to mother nature!"

Mia frowned. So they'd be sleeping on the ground, in sleeping bags. "Uh . . . okay."

"First, we must wash up, to keep our tent as clean as possible," Barbie said.

They each grabbed a metal pail from the side of the tent. Holly handed one to her. "I had this made up for you."

"Thank you," Mia said, looking inside. There was a small towel, a sliver of cracked soap that had been so worn down that it was almost see-through, and a half-used tube of toothpaste. She followed them to an outdoor station, where there were several outdoor spigots depositing water into a single large trough. Beyond that, there were two stations, surrounded by white sheets.

"Those are the showers," Barbie said when she noticed her looking. "But most of the time we just wash up in the sinks. It's faster that way."

So they did. Mia did just as the others did, using handfuls of water to pat on her face and body. The soap was so hard that it didn't lather. It felt like a cat-wash. By the time she was done, she didn't feel much cleaner, but she was shivering even more. And she didn't have a toothbrush, so she had to put the paste on her finger, swish it around, and hope for the best.

"Ah, that feels so much better!" Holly said as they walked back.

By now, Mia had noticed the fire was waning, but the men were singing songs and laughing loudly. They sounded like drunken frat boys. "What do those men do for their jobs?" she asked as they walked past.

Holly looked at them as if she'd never seen them before, and tilted her head. "Why do you ask?"

"Well, they've been sitting around the fire ever since dinner ended. So I just wondered—"

"They have very important jobs. I assure you," Barbie said briskly. "But we shouldn't hang around here, gawking at them. It's not a woman's place to do that."

A woman's place? She hadn't heard anyone say anything like that since. . . well, never. She'd become an FBI agent, for God's sake. If anyone had told her it was not a woman's place to be one, she would've smacked them upside the head. But no one was so backwards, like that, anymore . . . or at least, that's what she'd thought. Until now.

Mia followed them back to the tent, placed her pail next to the others, and watched as Holly climbed in.

Barbie tweaked her side. "Don't worry. It's plenty cozy. Plus, it's really only temporary until the new cabins are constructed."

Seemed like a lot of things about this place were *only temporary.* How many times had she heard the excuse, *Growing pains* since she got here? A hundred, at least.

Luckily, though, the tent was roomier from the inside. Barbie handed her a bedroll, which she spread out in the only open area of the tent. Once that was set out, there was no open area to crawl around, unless you wanted to step on someone. She sat down on the bedroll, shivering and wondering if she'd be able to sleep.

"Here," Barbie said, crawling over to her with an extra blanket. She laid it beside her and opened a jar. Mia could barely see it in the minimal light from an overhead camping lantern, but it smelled sweet, like aloe. "This is the best stuff for just about everything."

Mia dipped her finger in and spread it over her nose. She expected it to burn, but it actually made the stinging go away. "Thank you."

She climbed under the covers, still shivering, and pulled the blankets up to her chin. It felt better, but she was still cold.

"Good night, girls," Barbie said, beginning to crawl out of the tent. "See you in the morning."

Mia sat up on her elbows. "Aren't you going to bed?"

"In a bit," she said, and disappeared.

Holly settled into her bag, smiling. Then she reached up and turned off the cabin light. Darkness swallowed them. Mia fell back into her bedroll, wishing she had a softer pillow. The ground was impossibly hard.

She rolled over and looked toward Holly, though she couldn't see anything. Barbie seemed a little bit more militant, but Mia thought she could get further with Holly, so this was perfect. "Where did she go?" Mia whispered.

Holly said, "Oh, it's Barbie! She's in high demand!" And she giggled.

Mia wasn't sure what that meant. "Okay . . ."

"She's one of the originals. So she always gets invited to the secret night meetings."

"Secret night meetings?"

"Yeah. They get together and discuss very high-level things from the community, to make sure they're keeping with the original aims of the community. Brother Brent is very aware of our needs and wants to make sure he's addressing all our concerns."

"You really like him," she observed. She could see that now. It wasn't just blowing smoke.

"Oh, my gosh, yes. He's the best. So kind, and competent, and handsome . . ." She let out a long breath. "So what did you think about everything, today?"

"It's great. Different. A lot to take in."

"Oh, yes, it is. I know, for the first week I was here, I kept doing everything wrong. I thought Barbie was going to skin me alive, she was so frustrated with me!" More giggles.

Mia forced a laugh, too. Then she turned serious. "I was actually hoping I'd find a couple of my friends here. They went off the grid years ago, and there was talk that they might have come here."

"Oh? What were their names?"

"Carrie and Madison," Mia said.

"They don't sound . . . " There was a pause, and then she took a deep breath. "Wait . . . I have heard their names before. Well, I heard something about a Sister Carrie, but she was here before I arrived. I've only been here a few years. And I don't know anything about a Madison, but someone had carved that name in the wash-house. On one of the posts? Most people probably can't even see it, but since I work there all the time, I was able to figure it out."

"Really? Like a secret message? You'll have to show me."

"Sure. But I'm sorry. They probably didn't make it through the trial period. I know they're not here, now."

"Hmm. That's too bad," Mia said, rolling over in bed. "Good night."

But it was progress. It meant that all three girls had been there before. And now that she knew she was in the right place, Mia just had to dig a little more. She was sure of it. In a couple days, if she asked the right questions, she'd have her answers.

*

The whistle blew before sunrise.

Mia sat up straight on her bedroll, in the midst of a dream that involved running through the desert, chasing after Aiden and Kelsey, always a few steps behind.

She blinked and looked around, unable to see anything until Holly reached up and turned on the overhead camp light. "Another great day!" she chirped.

As Mia's eyes adjusted to the light, she noticed Barbie was there, as well. Though Mia didn't think she'd slept very well, apparently, after all that walking the day before, she'd been so out of it last night that she hadn't even heard Barbie return. Barbie quickly scrambled out of bed and said, "Come on, Sister Danielle. We need to get an early start. No work for you today, but we'll show you the ropes, at least."

"Thanks," she said, pushing off her warm covers. It was still cold out, and her body screamed to go back under the blankets, but she couldn't. She followed them out, and once again, they went to wash up.

As they walked, she noticed women coming out of tents. Just the women. At the wash station, it was all women, again, so many of them that it was hard to get a space in front of the sink. So where were the men? Was it not a man's place to help do the morning chores?

"Where is everyone?" Mia asked casually, managing to get her hand under the faucet so she could splash some water on her face.

"If you mean the men, they get up an hour after we do." Barbie motioned to the sink. "If we were all fighting to get ready at once, it'd be a free-for-all. We're planning on adding to the wash stations, though, next month. Gr--"

"Growing pains, I got it," Mia said.

"Your nose looks much better," Barbie said, pointing and beaming. "My secret formula."

Mia touched it. Sure enough, it didn't hurt as much. "Wow. That's great."

"See, you don't need the medical tent for everything," she added.

Holly frowned and said, "Especially since they only see—"

Barbie nudged her, and she yelped and shut up.

Mia waited, hoping one of them would finish the thought, but neither did. "Since they only see what?"

Barbie blinked. "Hmm?"

"Holly just said they only see . . . what was she talking about?"

"Oh. They only like to see people during certain hours, that's all," Barbie said, dismissively. "Last night, it was so late, I didn't want to bother them."

"I thought Holly said that they were on call during all hours of the night?"

Barbie sighed. "Yes, they are, but I wouldn't want to wreck anyone's sleep for a little sunburn."

And yet you two worked until midnight to make sure everyone had clean towels this morning, Mia thought.

Mia asked, "So what is the schedule like for this morning? Do we do morning chores, first, or have breakfast?"

"We have morning chores, like I mentioned," Barbie said as they piled their things into their pails and headed back to the tent. "Gathering all the dirty laundry and setting out the clean in every tent. Once we get done with that, we'll meet the men in the mess hall for breakfast."

"Oh," Mia said, looking around as the other women headed off to their own work. "Seems like the laundry people have the longest job!"

"No, that's not really true," Holly piped up. "The girls in charge of the garden and the storeroom are busy all the time, and the medical assistants are on call, twenty-four hours a day. We're actually lucky."

"What about the men?" Mia blurted.

Barbie turned to her, a strange look on her face, but then smiled. "I told you. They all have important jobs, too."

But I don't ever actually see them doing them! They get to party early, sleep late . . . what am I missing?

She kept that to herself, as they headed to the wash house. There, she watched as the women scooped the fresh linens and towels into baskets, which they carried on their heads. After she lifted hers, Holly winked at Mia and pointed to the wooden pole that was the main support of the tent.

Mia squinted, turning her head to the side. Sure enough, in small, block letters, carved into the post on a diagonal, it said, *MADISON WAS HERE.*

She almost ran a finger over it but then Barbie called to her, "Come on, Sister Danielle. The day's a wasting! We have lots of deliveries to finish!"

Quickly Mia scurried to keep up with them, and stayed with them as they made their deliveries. As they walked down the main area, the sun was coming up over the horizon, brilliant and orange. She noticed more tents opening up, and the men coming out, bare-chested, pulling their overalls up over their shoulders and greeting the rapidly warming day.

Well, that guy has a pretty big tent. Hope it's not just him in there, Mia thought bitterly, trying not to stare. The tent was probably five times the size of the one she'd been forced to share with two people. That hardly seemed fair.

But a moment later, another thought hit her.

Hadn't she seen a woman coming out of that tent, a little while ago?

Convinced she'd probably made a mistake, or that maybe there were tents for married people, she continued on her way. Yes, that was probably it. Married people.

"How many married couples come to this place?" she asked Holly as they stopped at a tent to drop off fresh towels.

"Couples?" She looked confused. "Oh, we don't have any couples."

"But I just . . ." She started to point to the tent but then saw another woman come out of it. One man . . . two women . . . who else would come out of that tent? What kind of crazy living arrangement was that? She was so busy staring, this time, that she nearly tripped over a rock in the middle of the path.

"Whoa, watch yourself!" a kind male voice said as she stumbled up against a hard body. Hands reached out and steadied her, warm on her still-cool skin. She straightened and looked up into the eyes of Brother Paul.

She tried to scramble away from him, but his hand stayed firmly planted on her waist. "I'm sorry—"

"No, no reason to be sorry, Sister Danielle," he said, pushing aside a lock of hair that had fallen into her face and sweeping it behind her ear. "It took us all a while to learn the lay of the land, didn't it, girls?"

Holly giggled. Barbie said, "Yes, it's nothing to be sorry about. We were all new here, once before. Even Brother Brent."

"So true, Sister Barbie. Now, Sister Danielle, how was your first night in our paradise?" he asked her, his eyes never leaving hers. "I trust you were in very good hands with these ladies. Did you sleep well?"

"Yes," she said, *Even though the ground was hard as hell and the tent was freezing. Thank goodness I walked almost 20 miles yesterday. That helped.* "It's nice being out here, in nature."

"Yes! Did you hear the coyotes calling?" He grinned. "And the cool desert air, it's so fresh and clean. There really is nothing like it."

She nodded.

"Well, that's wonderful." He broke his gaze from her, though he kept his hand locked on her hip. "These two busy little bees have been showing you all about laundry service, eh? An important job. A very important job. We couldn't survive without it. My hat's off to you."

Mia nodded, noting that he was now stroking her hip lightly with his fingertips. That was odd. What was he up to? She didn't have to guess. She didn't *want* to guess. Of all the people she'd met so far, Brother Paul definitely had the creepiest vibe. She squirmed the slightest bit, and it had the desired effect, because he finally let go. "It's very interesting," she said, trying to come up with something positive. "I love how everything works like clockwork. There's no guessing as to what I should be doing at any moment. It's so—"

"Simple, right?" Holly said with giggle. "I know. It's nice that way. It helps you appreciate every little blessing in life."

Barbie nodded. "Yes, and we have so many blessings here. Too many to count."

They all nodded.

Paul held up a finger. "Speaking of blessings, that reminds me. Girls, can you spare your new helper for a bit?" Now, he put a hand on her shoulder.

What did he want? From the way he was touching her and looking at her, alarms were going off in her head, and they all pointed to something bad. One thing was for sure-- she did not want to be alone with Brother Paul. She began to babble, "Why take me away from them? I actually haven't been helping them at all yet, and I have so much to learn—"

"Brother Brent would like to speak with you."

Her stomach dropped. That was even worse. Strike what she'd thought before—Paul was creepy, but Brother Brent was the head creep in charge. He wanted to see her? Why?

"What is this all about? I just--"

"He just wants to have a private word with you. That's all."

Mia gritted her teeth, wondering what that meant. She looked over at Barbie, hoping she'd say that she couldn't spare her, but Barbie simply nodded.

"Of course," Barbie said, and they spun and continued on with their work.

"Good. Come quickly. Brother Brent does not like to be kept waiting." Brother Paul clamped the hand on her shoulder hard and nudged her toward the office. Mia allowed herself to be led away, wondering if this meeting meant that she was in trouble.

CHAPTER EIGHTEEN

More alarm bells went off in Mia's head, the moment they separated from her roommates. She realized at that moment that he wasn't leading her in the direction of Brent's office.

She hesitated. "Where are we going?"

"Come with me," he said shortly. He seemed a little annoyed that she kept asking questions. "I just have to make a stop before delivering you to the office."

She couldn't help it, though. Creepy Paul was starting to really freak her out. "A stop, where?"

This time, he didn't answer, which made her pulse race. She was worried that he'd take her into some tent somewhere, away from everyone else, and try something. If he did that, she'd have to use the boxing skills she'd learned at Quantico to defend herself, and that would likely give her away, or at the very least, make her an enemy. She couldn't afford either. She had to be careful.

But she didn't have to worry. He stopped at the gate she'd come through, fished in the pockets of his overalls for a key, and started to work a thick padlock that had been chained around the gate. That was curious. There hadn't been a lock yesterday, when she'd arrived.

"You locked the gate?" she asked, wincing. Another question. He'd probably ignore her again.

But he answered, "Of course. At night. For our safety. We don't want any outsiders coming in without our knowledge."

Or you don't want anyone getting out? "Then why don't you leave it locked all the time?"

He gave her a curious look. "Because this is not a prison. Besides, Sister Danielle, we're expecting some supply trucks from the outside today. They should be here any moment."

"Oh."

He wound the chain up, then pocketed the key, spun on his heel and headed purposefully toward the main office building. Mia rushed to keep up with his long strides but wound up trailing behind him like a tail.

She struggled to avoid bits of gravel in her path, the soles of her bare feet burning on the already hot, cracked earth. She was glad when she finally reached the shaded refuge of the porch.

When she looked up, Paul was waiting for her, his expression stern. “Don’t lag. Brother Brent hates to be kept waiting.”

“I’m not. I’m just not used to walking in bare feet.”

He looked down. “Ah, yes, that takes some getting used to. But you’ll find that once you toughen up your soles, shoes really become an unnecessary nuisance.”

“But what if I like shoes?” she asked. “I’m not allowed to have them?”

He opened the door and looked back at her. “When you join our community, you may sacrifice things for a certain way of life. The way of life we espouse. If you don’t like it, you’re more than willing to start your own community, where people wear shoes.”

She blinked. *Okay, that was a little harsh.* But she probably deserved it, for questioning everything. *Mia, stop being the fly in the ointment. If you don’t at least try to fit in, you’re not going to get to the bottom of what happened to those girls.*

“I understand. I was just wondering,” she said lightly, as he led her to the back of the house. The air conditioning was churning out icy air, making her shiver in her slight shift.

He took her into an office that was decorated with a very masculine hunter green and deep mahogany, with paintings and décor of ducks, everywhere. Brent was sitting behind a very large, very official-looking desk, like that of a banker. It was completely out of place, considering no one outside his office was even allowed to wear shoes.

He looked up from the papers he was reading and removed his wire-rimmed spectacles. “Ah, if it isn’t our newest family member, Sister Danielle!” he said, standing to greet her. He shook her hand with both of his and motioned for her to sit in a leather chair, across from him.

She sat down, feeling woefully underdressed.

“So, we’re all dying to know,” he said, exchanging a glance with Paul, who lingered in the doorway. “How was your first night with us? Pleasant, I hope?”

She nodded. “Great. Really, just wonderful.”

He raised an eyebrow, which made her wonder if she’d gone a little too far with the gushing. “Sure about that? Anything you didn’t like?”

"Well, I'm not used to sleeping on the ground."

"And the bare feet thing," Paul piped up.

"Right. But it'll just take a little getting used to." She smiled.

"So, you're willing to? No hesitations?" When she nodded, he gave her two thumbs up. "This is good news. We're so happy to have you."

He grabbed a piece of paper and prepared to write.

"Now," he said, scribbling something down. "As I mentioned, there is the importance of work around here. We'll start you with light duty. As you know, it's not an easy lifestyle; we work for almost everything we have, farm our own food, build what we need. Once a week, we have a truck come in that delivers the essential supplies we can't make on our own. I'm writing down instructions for Barbie, so she knows how to settle you in. Sound good?"

"Yes," she said, as he folded he paper and handed it to Paul. "But I was wondering if you might have a moment to discuss something I heard among the women last night. Something private."

His smile fell. He nodded. "Brother Paul, go ahead and take this to Barbie. Close the door behind you, so that Sister Danielle and I might speak in private."

Paul nodded obediently and stepped out.

Brent laced his fingers in front of him. "Now, what is it? Something serious?"

"I believe so," she said, leaning in. "I've been talking to the other women, at dinner, and they mentioned a few women that were part of Rising Sun, but left. Rachel was one of them, but there were two more, from a few years earlier."

"Rachel . . .," he mused, testing out the name. "Yes, I do remember the name. She was here for a few months, until just a week ago?"

"That's correct."

He smiled. "Yes, as I mentioned, this way of life isn't for everyone. It can be hard. From what I remember, Rachel took issue with all the rules. She complained a lot. And eventually, she decided to leave us. It's unfortunate, but it happens. We always hate to lose a sister."

"Unfortunate?" She almost laughed. That was an understatement. "It's horrible, that's what it is. The way she died?"

His eyes narrowed. "I'm sorry?"

She stared at him, trying to understand. Did he really not know? "She was found murdered, her body burned, at Phantom Bridge, not far from here."

Now, his eyes grew wide. “What?” He coughed. “Oh, my. Are you sure?”

“Yes, the police identified her. I only brought it up because I was wondering about her, and the women told me she’d been here, before.”

He was growing paler by the moment. “That’s extraordinary. And the police don’t have any suspects?”

“No. But it does seem similar to two murders that happened, several years ago. Carrie Winters and Madison Lane.”

He choked again, and clasped at his heart. “They were killed in the same way?”

She nodded, watching him closely. The man was genuinely shocked by the news. If he knew about or had a hand in Rachel’s murder, he was a very good liar. “Set on fire and left for dead in the desert.”

“Goodness . . . that’s terrible.”

“Do those names ring a bell?” she asked carefully.

His mouth opened slightly, and his breath caught. “I . . . I don’t know. It was some years ago, you said? I can’t say I remember . . .”

That’s bull. You said you knew every new family member. You remember them. You’re just not willing to tell me that.

“Oh, well,” she added with a shrug. “But you can see why I’m a little hesitant.”

His shock cleared, and he nodded. “Of course. But I can assure you, nothing like that will happen again. We keep our flock safe, and as long as you are with us, you won’t have to worry about anything like that.”

Right, but it’s what happens when someone leaves that I’m worried about. “I noticed that you locked the gates, at night?”

He nodded. “Right. We had a couple of situations, in the past, where certain unwanted people tried to get in. So for our safety—”

“So I *can’t* leave anytime.”

He stopped and tilted his head. “What?”

“Well, you said that anyone could leave at any time. But that isn’t really true, because the gates are locked,” she said, smiling when she realized she was doing it again, challenging them when she needed to simply fall in line and behave.

“Yes, but . . . Sister Danielle. I don’t think you’d want to leave in the dead of night. We would wonder where you went! At least, I would hope you’d do us the courtesy of trying to work things out with us, first?”

“Yes, I would, but—"

“There are all types of people outside those gates. You’re the one who should know that best, considering what you just brought up with those three women.” He tapped his pen on the desk. “I can’t be responsible for what happens outside these gates. What I can do is assure our people that I have their best interests at heart. You see?”

She nodded. “I see. I was just clarifying. Thank you. That’s all.”

“All right.” He looked back at his papers, which she assumed was a dismissal. “Sister Danielle, let me reiterate that we’re all thrilled to have you as a part of our little slice of heaven. Should you run into any more concerns like the one you just voiced to me, please, don’t hesitate to bring it before me. That’s what I’m here for.”

He smiled widely, a smile that made shivers run down her back.

She turned and headed out to the wash-house, deep in thought.

Brother Brent had known those dead girls. All of them. That, Mia was sure about. But what he hadn’t known was that they’d all been murdered. Now, she wondered if, as the newcomer and bearer of that bad news, she’d unwittingly brought trouble upon herself.

CHAPTER NINETEEN

"Light duty! *Light* duty!" Barbie squawked from the corner of the wash-house as Mia scrubbed another pair of dirty overalls. She was getting into a rhythm, breaking a sweat, because she was so deep in thought about her conversation with Brother Brent.

Holly giggled next to her as she hung a few more tunics on the indoor drying line. "You're washing up a storm!"

"Well, I'm not taking it any easier than you two were! I'm just trying to get this stuff done!" Mia said.

Holly laughed. "Well, we appreciate it. For the first time, I think we might be done before dinner. That would be nice, wouldn't it, Barbie?"

Barbie shot her a look. "No, if we were, then I think we should take on additional duties. We wouldn't want to be slacking off, now, would we?"

"Like the men?" Mia asked.

Both women stared at her.

She shrugged. "I don't know. I just haven't seen the men doing very much work. That's all," she pointed out.

"What the men do is really no concern of yours," Barbie said sharply. "But if you must know, they have important jobs and different shifts. Just because you might not see them working doesn't mean they aren't working."

Mia sighed. "I guess. I just—"

"It's all right," Barbie said, as if she were a child. She approached her. "Let me see your hands."

Mia pulled them out of the water and presented them to the older woman. They were pruned red, and the beginning of a blister was showing on the pad of one of her fingers. The woman tutted.

"Take it easy, now. You're going to get me in trouble with Brother Brent! I promised him that I would take it easy on you," she hissed, her voice low. "Let me take over with the wash. You check the clothing outside and see if it's dry yet. If it is, bring it in, and I'll give you some more to hang."

She left her spot behind the washtub and went out to the front of the tent, a strange feeling overcoming her. Working hard like that must've released endorphins, because despite being tired, she felt content, like she used to after a five-mile run. She felt better than she had in a long time, probably because she didn't have to worry about the police being on her tail. And truthfully, out here, in the middle of nowhere, cut off from regular society, was the perfect place to be if she wanted to hide out.

But though it had some perks, though it brought her a sense of security from the world outside, she knew it had to be only temporary. First and foremost, she had to get back to her family. She needed to stop spinning her wheels and concentrate.

Something pulled at her as she stepped into the scalding sun of late morning. Of course, the tunics they'd put out there only moments before were already dry. It was stifling and stuffy in the tent, but it had to be at least 115 degrees in the sun. Wiping the sweat from her brow, she removed the clothespins and piled the garments into the basket.

As she was working on the last few, she heard the sound of tires on gravel. Looking up, shielding her eyes from the sun, she noticed a white truck, rumbling up the center of the village. People stepped aside as it slowly made its way to the office.

Mia strained to see past the windshield. It was a young man, in a backwards baseball cap, with long, stringy dark hair. Other than that, she couldn't see much. As it drove on, she noticed the Texas license plate: JGT-478.

She missed having her phone. If she had it, she'd have taken a photo of it. Instead, she made a mental note of it, just in case it meant something.

My phone. She really wished she had that on her. She'd spend a good amount of time wondering if David or Marcus had tried to be in touch with her. Not that she wanted them to—it would be bad if Marshal Kane Wilcox got wind of it and somehow traced it down here. But though it was safer here, she had to wonder if there had been any more developments in the case. Had David Hunter found anything new? What was Wilson Andrews doing?

She had to face the facts, though. As far as clearing her name went, everything was at a standstill. Where she was concerned, all law enforcement wanted was to get her back in custody. She was the only one capable of proving her innocence. And here? She couldn't do much of that.

Her fingers itched at the thought. She had to make things happen here, soon, so she could get back to Dallas and continue her search.

She grabbed the last tunic and stuffed it in the basket, then picked it up and started back into the tent. As she did, she noticed a large, round-bellied man with a receding hairline, sitting on a pail in the shade near the mess hall tent, wiping the sweat from his brow.

"Hey, girl," he said, waving at her.

Mia stiffened, wanting to ignore him and continue with her duties.

But he called again, louder still. "Girl. Come on over here."

She took a step toward him and said, "I can't, I'm in the middle of—"

"What's your name?"

She faltered for a moment before remembering her alias. "Danielle."

"Danielle," he spoke the word slow, savoring every syllable. Then he lips spread into a grin. He was missing a front tooth, and his other teeth were a sick yellow. He scratched at his belly. "You're new, here, right? I saw you come in yesterday."

I didn't see you. But I wasn't missing much, she thought. She nodded and tried to head off, but he spoke again.

"I'm Todd."

She gave him a slight smile. "Nice to meet you," she said tightly, trying to back away.

"It's really nice to meet you, Sister Danielle," he said, rubbing the side of his belly in a suggestive way. "Really nice. I'm going to keep my eye on you, girl."

Mia's stomach lurched. "Well, you can keep your eye on me as I go in the tent over here and finish my work," she said, finally backing off.

"I will," he said, and because of that, she refused to turn around. She backed into the tent, bumping her head on a pole, as he added, "I'll see you soon, sweet girl."

Nausea bubbled in her throat, and had nothing to do with the oppressive heat. She really hoped she wouldn't see him soon. She couldn't take any more distractions if she wanted to look into this case any further. She dipped her head under the tent and went inside, deciding that she'd have to start asking more questions, faster, to make something happen.

Inside, Barbie said, "If we do have time this evening, we should work on patching the older garments that have tears and holes. You do know how to sew, don't you, Sister Danielle?"

Mia nodded, though the extent of her knowledge was learned in eighth grade home economics class and rarely boiled down to more than sewing a missing button on a coat, these days.

Sewing. That's just what I want to do tonight. Sew a bunch of old clothes.

But it did make her wonder—did women ever get time to just relax? Or was it work, work, work, all the day long? And even when they ran out of things to do, were more things just piled onto their plate? That sounded . . . hellish.

Just then, the lunch whistle blew. Mia dropped her basket on a table. "Let's go."

Barbie continued to wash. "In a few minutes."

Mia groaned, and her stomach groaned along with her. They'd gotten to breakfast late after their chores, so though the men had eggs, most of the women had been stuck with a simple scoop of tasteless porridge. It had been rather unsatisfying.

"I'm a little hungry," she said. "Maybe I'll just go . .."

Holly cast her a warning look. Barbie said, "No. Not until you finish folding those clothes in that basket. If you don't fold them, they'll be wrinkled, and we can't have wrinkles, can we?"

Mia looked down at the basket on the table. It would take at least twenty minutes to fold all that. And that meant . . . they'd be late to a meal, again, and probably only get the scraps.

But for the first time, she realized that it seemed that was exactly what Sister Barbie wanted. That it was part of a bigger plan . . . for what?

Despite being away from the law enforcement that was hunting her down, no. Mia didn't feel safe here at all.

CHAPTER TWENTY

Please God, please God, please God . . .

Lola's heart leapt into her throat as she murmured the prayer. She heard the engine of the delivery truck rumble to life. Crouched in her hiding spot, she smiled as she felt the truck begin to move.

So close. She was so close.

Suddenly, though, the brakes squealed, and the truck came to a stop. A voice outside the truck shouted, "Wait! Someone wants to have a word with you."

She held her breath as she heard the driver say, "Yep! No problem! Take your time."

More waiting.

She'd been tucked away here for what felt like ages. It hadn't been hard to crawl into the truck. She'd simply told the girls at the storeroom that she needed to use the restroom, and then, when the coast was clear, she'd gotten the thumbs-up from the driver, and jumped into the back of the truck and hidden behind a few milk crates.

But now, her palms were slick with sweat. If the truck didn't move soon, the others at the storeroom would start to wonder where the hell she'd gone. And then they'd start looking for her.

She'd been vocal about her hate for this place. Barbie said she was too vocal, and needed to shut up, "if she knew what was good for her."

Good for her. Lola knew what was good for her. And it sure as hell wasn't this place.

She needed this truck to get moving. Now.

But that dumb-as-a-stump kid who was driving the truck seemed to be taking his sweet time. He chatted with someone out there, shooting the breeze. Then it seemed like there was something missing from the list—a missing carton of yeast from town, it sounded like. They were supposed to have twelve boxes and only counted eleven. Someone—it sounded like Vera from the cooking tent, was having a fit. Even from her hiding place, Lola could hear Vera's screeching voice, barely muffled by the old sacks she'd thrown over her body to conceal herself.

"I'll count it again, but I'm pretty sure you're missing one!" Vera said.

Missing one . . . oh, God, Vera. Shut up, for once in your life.

"Don't bother. I'll add it to the list and bring you more next week," the driver told her.

"No, that won't be good, we'll run out by the end of the week if you do that," she responded. "I think I should tell Brother Brent and have you come back later."

"Hey, lady, I can't come back later," he told her, annoyed. "Don't be crazy. I got a thousand more deliveries after this one. You're gonna have to wait 'til next—"

"No, no, no! You stay right here. I'm gonna get Brother Brent!"

Oh, no, Lola thought. *Leave it to Vera to screw everything up. I'm toast.*

"What's the commotion here?" a male voice said. Brother Paul.

Lola swallowed as she listened to Vera explain the issue and how Brother Brent would be upset and want the delivery truck to return. Meanwhile, Lola thought she might throw up. It was so hot back here, and she was getting dizzy.

Brother Paul simply said, "We should have enough yeast if you ration it to last the week." He banged on the side of the truck. "Go on, driver. We'll see you next week."

Of course, that was the Rising Sun way. Ration everything, even if people went without meals. But for the first time, Lola was glad for Paul's ruling. As second-in-command, Vera would have no choice but to listen to him.

And sure enough, she did. Lola let out a sigh of relief as the truck again began to lumber on its way. *Thank God. Get me away from this hellhole.*

She allowed her heart to skip with excitement over what she'd left behind. No longer would she have to go through cans of supplies, setting aside the best ones for certain people. No longer would she have to lie to people's faces. No longer would she have to work from morning until night with barely a break, only for a few scraps of food in return. No longer would she have to see him.

She would be free. So soon, she could almost taste it.

She listened as the truck slowed a bit, and heard the gate creaking open. Then the truck rumbled forward, picking up speed.

She'd done it. She'd escaped from him. *Thank God,* she thought again, clasping her hands in front of her and praying for the truck to put more distance between her and that nightmare.

Funny, when she'd arrived there, eighteen months ago, she'd thought it was so good. She was escaping a possessive boyfriend who'd constantly kept tabs on her, and a minimum-wage job that could barely put food on the table. She'd just been served an eviction notice because they hadn't been able to make rent for the sixth month in a row, and her car was constantly breaking down. Everything in her life had been shit.

She'd heard of places like Rising Sun—communities where people were family, working together, caring for one another. It had sounded like heaven. So she'd gotten on the web and quickly found out about this place. She'd driven straight through the night from Missouri, making it into Bracketville on fumes. And when she'd arrived, she thought her troubles were over.

How wrong she'd been. She'd simply traded a bad situation for an even worse one.

She shuddered at the thought of him and hugged herself tighter. No more. She was free.

Just as she had been instructed, the truck finally slowed to a stop.

She climbed to her feet then opened up the back door and squinted in the bright sunlight. Her orders were to climb out when the truck stopped. So she did, her bare feet hitting the dusty ground.

The truck lumbered on, the driver never looking back.

When it moved off, she spun in a circle, scanning her surroundings. Nothing but desert, as far as she could see.

This couldn't be right. There was supposed to be someone here to help her. That was the plan.

She gnawed on her lip as she spun around, then hugged herself, a chill gripping her despite the sweltering temperatures. She had no shoes. Barely any clothing. No water, no food. If the plans fell through, if no one was here to help her . . .

To her relief, she saw a figure approaching on the dirt road, from the direction of Bracketville.

Oh, thank God! she thought for the thousandth time that day. Maybe things would work out after all. She'd been told that her contact would provide her with clothes, shoes, and enough necessities so that she could get a start in life. She could hitch a ride away from here. Not to that abusive boyfriend of hers, though. She'd start completely fresh.

Get a job. Find a place to live. She'd find a way to survive, just like she always did.

When the figure neared her, she noticed it was a man. She'd never seen him before. He was wearing a trucker's cap and a flannel shirt, jeans, and work boots despite the heat. He had a backpack slung over his shoulder.

"Lola?" he asked as he neared.

She smiled. It felt so good to have someone call her Lola, and not Sister Lola. How ridiculous was that? They'd told her they treated their own like family, but it was all bullshit. You didn't do that to family. "Yes."

He opened his backpack and took out a bottle of water, which he handed to her. "Great. I'm here to help you."

"Thank you so much," she said, near tears, as she took the water. It wasn't cold, but the condensation on the label suggested it had once been. She sucked back a huge mouthful, then another. It tasted heavenly, compared to the sludge they passed off as water in The Rising Sun.

He pulled his hat off his head, then screwed it on tighter. "All right. Come on. We can't stay here in one place for long."

He started to lead her off toward the mountains. Away from the town of Bracketville.

Lola stared after him, confused. "Aren't we going to town?"

He stopped and turned around. "Nope. I've got a vehicle out this way. Got some shoes for you and some supplies, too."

"Okay."

She followed as he walked her toward the mountains. After a few steps, she shielded her eyes from the sun with her hand and squinted, trying to see his car. Everything in the distance seemed to bleed together. She could see nothing.

"I'm sorry," she said after they'd walked a few more steps. "I don't see anything that way."

He didn't answer. He continued to walk, until she was several paces behind him. She paused there, wondering if she should trust him. After what she'd been through, she didn't have faith in many people. But as she looked around, she realized it didn't matter. If she went off on her own, she'd never make it to civilization.

For the first time, she began to wonder if this was a mistake.

She'd been so eager to leave the commune that she'd grabbed hold of the first opportunity that was presented to her. She hadn't really thought it through.

And now . . . now, her life was in this man's hands. She had no choice.

So she skipped into a run, despite the pain on the soles of her feet from the uneven terrain. She caught up with him. "Where are we going?" she asked again.

Again, no answer.

He wouldn't hurt her, though. Everything was going her way. She'd escaped. The worst was over. *I'm sure of it,* she told herself, mostly to keep her nerves in check.

But he went over to a large boulder on the side of the dirt path and pulled something out.

A can of fuel. A book of matches.

She stopped walking and stared at it. What on earth did he need that for?

Then, he pulled out a long knife.

And he began to advance on her.

She stared at the blade for a split second before she began to scream. But she already knew that no one would hear her. She thought of running away, but she already knew there was nowhere to go. The only thing she knew for sure was that she was entirely dependent on this man, and he could do with her whatever he pleased.

And so, she closed her eyes and did the only thing she could. She began to pray.

CHAPTER TWENTY ONE

Sure enough, by the time Mia and the laundry crew had finished with their work, all that was available for lunch was more rice. Just as during previous meals, all the men sat in the front, taking leisurely meals. They all had hamburgers—some, two of them. But Mia made it a point of looking at all the women's plates, and there wasn't a single burger to be found, there.

As Mia used her finger to pick up every last grain of rice from her plate, she looked around at the men, chowing down on their big, juicy burgers, and her stomach rumbled.

"This rice is really . . . great," she whispered to the old lady, Charlie, "I guess it serves us right, for being late. We missed out on the best food again."

Charlie shook her head. "They wouldn't let you have it, even if you were early. They always make excuses. I haven't had meat in two years."

Mia eyed her in shock. "Are you serious?"

Charlie nodded meekly, but cast her eyes to the side and didn't say more. Mia glanced over and noticed Barbie watching them carefully.

Barbie said, "Sometimes there are shortages. But it's really not all that bad, considering what we get in return."

The women nodded along with her.

Mia pushed her plate away. As she did, she noticed the man, Todd, walking past. His eyes were glued to her. He licked his lips and winked.

The rice in her stomach threatened to make a reappearance. The man was slovenly and repulsive.

Holly leaned over and elbowed her. "I see Todd has taken an interest in you, you lucky girl."

Mia looked at her, trying to gauge if she was serious. "Yeah. Really. Lucky me."

"Well, he's one of the better catches in the commune," Holly whispered with a smile. "He's an original, so he has status, if you know what I mean."

She really didn't. Did status mean that he got two hamburgers? Weren't they all supposed to be equal, working for the common good? "I really would rather he not take an interest in me, thanks," she said wrinkling her nose.

Holly's eyes went wide. "Why not?"

"Well, because . . .," she shrugged. "I just got out of a bad relationship."

She giggled. "But it's totally not like that. The best thing you can do around here is get in with one of the originals. I'm telling you. You'll reap the rewards."

"What rewards?"

"Oh, easier work, more status, things like that. They get away with so much."

"Barbie's an original, though, and all she does is—"

"She's also a woman." Holly gave her a look like, duh. "Anyway, if I were you, I'd go for it with ol' Todd."

"Go for it . . .?" She repeated the words, trying to understand their meaning. But the thought made her queasy. "You mean— sleep with him?"

She laughed. "I mean, let him take you as his wife!"

Now, she really felt sick. "Why would I . . ."

"Well, there's way worse families to be part of. It'd be like marrying into royalty. If he had an interest in me, I'd totally jump on that train." She sighed and motioned with her chin to a rather handsome-looking younger man at the end of the row. "I got stuck with Jeff over there."

She dragged her hands down her face. "I don't understand . . . what's wrong with Jeff?"

"Nothing, on the surface. He's nice, I guess. But his others are constantly bickering, so that whenever we all get together, it always ends up in a fight."

"His others?"

She nodded. "His wives."

Mia sat there, her mouth slowly dropping open. Wives. Suddenly, it all seemed to fall into place. "You mean . . . polygamous?"

She laughed. "Did you not know that?"

"No! No one mentioned that to me at all!"

Holly shrugged. "Well, I guess that makes sense. It's only a small part of the core of our community. And I know, it was a little shocking to me, too. But it's actually a good thing, though. It makes the family stronger. It's helpful to shed the old notions of family that you might have brought with you. A man's duty is to take care of his family. And so that's a large part of what these men do. Which is why you don't see them engaged in much of the physical labor. They're managing the household. Their wives and children."

Mia felt like the earth beneath her was shaking. In no way could she ever justify this as a good thing.

"And I really feel bad for him," Holly was saying, though Mia wasn't paying attention. "He's lost wives before. One of his wives just recently left, so he has an opening."

Holly's words suddenly registered in Mia's head. *One of his wives just recently left.*

Rachel.

Her heart caught in her throat at the thought. There was a very good chance that Rachel had been married off to that man. And if anyone had an idea as to what had happened to Rachel . . . her husband could likely provide those answers.

She got up from the table without a word and went to the front of the tent. Then, she walked over to the tent near the wash-house. Sure enough, he was sitting outside it, in the shade. He had what looked like ketchup in his whiskers, and down the front of his overalls. Wiry gray hair poked from the top of the bib, matted with sweat.

"Todd?" she asked.

A slow smile spread over his face. "Sister Danielle. Couldn't keep away, could you?"

"You're right," she said, forcing a smile. "I couldn't. Do you mind if we talk, in private?"

He motioned to his tent, a question on his face, and she nodded.

"By all means," he said with a charming drawl. "I'm all ears for a lovely young lady such as yourself."

Mia's skin crawled as he held the tent flap open to let her pass through. But she swallowed back her disgust. She was determined to leave his tent with the information she needed.

CHAPTER TWENTY TWO

David Hunter clapped his hands from the sidelines. “That’s it, Louie! Way to hustle!”

Louie raised his head and looked over at his father, confusion marring his face. His expression seemed to say, *What are you cheering for, Dad? It’s only a practice.*

He gave him an encouraging thumbs-up.

But really . . . when had Louie gotten so good? David tried to make as many games as he could, but he must’ve missed a few. More than a few. Somehow, his son had gotten damn good, without him. Louie was on the ball, all the time. At bat, he’d hit a few out of the park. He was clearly the star player of the team.

How did he never notice this before?

Well . . . he’d had his reasons. A job that kept him constantly hustling, himself.

He looked over at the other parents, who were busy with their noses in their phones, or chatting with one another about school events. David had actually never stayed at a practice. He had a family friend take Louie to these things.

But since Pembroke had dropped that bomb on him, David had found himself with an abundance of free time. And being here was his way of making up for any lost time.

His mind was constantly going to the job, though. He kept thinking of all the cases that were now being handled by Anderson, and probably languishing. Anderson was late-fifties, with one foot in retirement—all he did was sit at his desk and make sure he was first in line for whatever treats were brought into the break room that day.

That was okay. He didn’t have to worry about Anderson showing him up. The cases would still be there when he got back, and then Pembroke would be sorry he ever made hm take that leave of absence.

He hoped. Unless they’d found something to connect him to Mia.

For the past few days, he’d been living in fear that they’d pound his front door down and arrest him. But the more time that passed, the safer he felt.

If only he could continue to help her. But that couldn't happen. He didn't have a phone to contact her. Had no clue where she was. And last he'd heard, Wilson Andrews had given the speech of a lifetime in University Park, and was now ahead in the polls by double-digits.

Mia wouldn't like that. Wherever she was.

But there was nothing he could do. He'd gradually resigned himself to that fact.

A kid hit a pop fly, and Louie shouted out, "I got it," and easily nabbed it. Hunter clapped once, then remembered it wasn't a game and shoved his hands into his pockets.

"David?" a voice said.

It was a blonde woman in a visor. One of the other parents. He couldn't remember her name, but she ran the PTA. "Hey. Yeah."

She smiled. "It's so good to see you! Darlene," she said, pointing to herself.

"Right. Yeah. Nice to see you, too."

"I just wanted to say hello. We don't usually see you here," she said, touching his arm. Her perfume made his eyes water. "Your boy is really one of the better players. My son, Alfie, too, is captain. Anyway, I was wondering if you'd be interested in going out for coffee one day?"

"Uh. . ." Was she asking him on a date? "Well—"

She spoke some more, and he tried to listen, but at that moment, a boy hit a ball that went foul. At first, David thought it might hit them, unbeknownst to Darlene, who was still chewing his ear off. He started to move her slightly, but no.

The ball fell short, hitting the ground at the trunk of a nearby oak tree by the water fountains.

That was when he noticed the man. He was standing there, wearing a baseball hat pulled low over his hair, and dark sunglasses . . . but David couldn't shake the feeling that his eyes were on him.

And he looked familiar. But with the clothes, he couldn't quite place him . . .

Wait. Was that Marcus Shields? The tech guy from his office?

What did he want?

Darlene was still talking, but David held up a finger. "I'm sorry. I have to go," he said, pulling free of her grip and jogging over to him.

As he approached, he said, "Shields. What's the—"

"Don't come closer. I think we're being watched. Just make like you're getting some water from the fountain and listen to me."

So they were going to play cloak and dagger? Interesting. Who was watching them? Probably that bastard, Wilcox. Doing as he was told, he walked casually to the nearby water fountain and stooped to take a drink.

"Mia's missing," he whispered.

Hunter chuckled between sips. "That's not news. She's on the run."

"You don't get it," he said through gritted teeth, looking around nonchalantly. "I got in touch with her and asked her to help me look into a case in Southwest Texas. My niece Rachel was murdered, and I thought she could help. She went there a few days ago, and since then . . . nothing. I've been calling her, pinging her phone, and it's showing up somewhere in the desert, but she's not answering. I think some serious shit is going down."

What the hell? As if Mia didn't have enough on her plate? He stopped drinking and straightened. "Are you fucking kidding me? Why would you do that to her?"

"Because she's the only one who could help. And—"

"And knowing Mia, she wouldn't turn that down. She probably jumped at the chance. Where did you send her?"

"Del Rio. But the phone was pinged to someplace outside of Bracketville."

"Del Rio? That's all the way on the other side of the world," he growled, wiping at his mouth. He'd never heard of Bracketville, but it was probably one of those shitty towns on the Mexican border. But of course, that wouldn't deter Mia. In fact, she'd probably thought it was a great idea to get out of town for a while, especially with that Wilcox guy closing in.

"Yeah. But she's missing. I don't know what happened. I heard you were on leave, so I thought . . ."

Hunter straightened, stretched his arms over his head, then bent down for another drink. "You thought wrong. You think you've got the Marshals on your ass? They're on mine, too. That's why I'm on leave."

"Shit. Isn't there anything we can do? I think she's in trouble."

It sounded like it. But what the hell could he do with them watching him? Their hands were tied. Except . . .

An idea rooted in his mind, and as it came together, he realized it was the only way.

“All right. Maybe neither of us can go check up on her. But I think I know someone who can.”

CHAPTER TWENTY THREE

Mia stepped into Todd's tent, and her jaw dropped.

Compared to the little camping tent she and the other women shared, this was a palace. It was constructed on a wooden platform, and two of the walls were made of wood planks, so the ceiling was high enough that she didn't have to stoop. There was a double bed in the corner, a dresser, and even a small makeshift kitchenette. He had a table and chairs in there, as well. "This is nice," she said, looking around.

He nodded proudly, still stroking the side of his round belly, and when he smiled, he stuck his tongue through the gap in his teeth. "I know, ain't it?"

"It's really impressive."

He went to the bed and laid out on it. "You like it, girl? Because if you play your cards right, all this could be yours to share with me."

"Is that so?" she said, managing a flirtatious smile. "I'm not sure how things work around here. So you have other wives, I'm told?"

He nodded. "Not as many as most. I lost a couple over the years. But I got room for one more. That's why I had my eye on you."

She patted her chest. "Me? I'm so flattered. But what happened to the wife you lost?"

Todd waved that away. "Ah. She wasn't happy. She wanted to leave. So she did. That's all."

"That's all?" she fixed him with a look, hoping he'd reveal more.

"Uh-huh." He patted the bed next to him. "Why don't you come here and join me, cutie?"

So he was going to do this the hard way. She looked around, then started to meander about the room. "Hold on, hold on. I'm taking everything in." She pointed to a photograph on the wall. It was the same one she'd seen in Brent's house. In it, she could immediately pick out Todd—he was younger, had more hair, but wasn't much thinner than he was now. "So you were here when it all began, huh? How did you know Brent? Were you from LA, too?"

He paused. “We ain’t supposed to talk about the old days. But yeah. I was a key grip on one of his films.” He patted the bed. “Come on over. Keep me company.”

She ignored him, pretending to be curious about everything in the room, to buy herself time. That was when she noticed the bread on the shelf. It was the same, stale stuff that they’d gotten crusts of in the mess hall, but he had an entire, giant loaf, under a dish rag. Next to it was a long, serrated bread knife.

“Hey, girlie, the whistle’s gonna blow soon. You don’t got much time before you’ll need to be back at work,” he said, his voice an octave high with his impatience.

She smiled back at him. “Oh, but an important person like you? You can make sure there’s an exception for me, right?”

He shook his head, his smile falling. “No. Ain’t no one able to make exceptions but Brent. You don’t want to be on his bad side, girl. I promise you that.”

“But you don’t even know me. And I want to know more about you!” she said, smiling. “It’s only right, if we’re going to bond in matrimony.”

Now, he was scowling. Clearly, he didn’t care about that. “Like what stuff do you want to know?”

Suddenly, the whistle blew, so loud that it made her jump. But that was her chance. In the next moment, she’d reached over and grabbed the knife. He was starting to complain that now she had to go, so he didn’t even see the blade until it was nearly pressed up against his fleshy neck.

“What are you . . . what are you doing?” Todd coughed out, eyes wide. “What the hell do you think you’re doing? Help!”

“I have a new arrangement for you. You shut up right now and I won’t make mincemeat out of your vocal cords. You understand?”

He gasped and held his breath. “What—what do you want?”

“I want the truth. What happened to your wife? The one that left?”

He shook his head frantically. “I don’t know! She left! She just left! I don’t know--”

“Her name was Rachel. Rachel Loring. And she died, alone and afraid in the desert. And I want to know what happened to her.”

He gasped, clearly shocked by the news. “I had no idea she died. I swear I don’t know! I swear! After she left, I never saw her again!”

"Don't bullshit me. She wanted to leave, and you couldn't stand that, so you killed her. And I bet you that you killed the other girls, too. I think they were your wives, as well!"

"No. I swear. I don't know. Rachel was my wife, yes. She was never happy, from the moment she got here. She wanted to leave. So we let her. That's all. That's all that happened with my other wives, too. I swear! They left."

"I don't believe you." She pressed the knife tighter against his throat.

Outside, someone shouted. Then, more voices joined in. She shifted and saw the shadows of bodies, running in a single direction. Something was going on outside.

She pulled the knife from his throat, leaving him gasping and clutching the blankets on his bed. "If you know what's good for you," she murmured to him, opening the flaps of the tent. "You'll keep this between you and me."

She ducked out of the tent, just as more people went running toward the front gate. Some were performing searches from tent to tent. Voices were raised, but she couldn't make out a single word in the commotion. Whatever it was, people were not happy about it.

She set the knife down and rushed into the chaos to see what was going on.

*

When Mia reached the front gate, she found Holly standing there, her hands pressed up against her cheeks, her mouth in the shape of an O.

"What's happening?" she asked.

"Oh, it's terrible!" she whispered, her voice barely a breath. "Lola—you remember her? She's missing!"

"Missing?" Mia cast her eyes around the area, where people were scattering like cockroaches. Now, she could hear some of them calling out Lola's name. "Since when?"

"They think it must've been around lunchtime. She works at the storeroom. She was there, right before the whistle. Then she excused herself to use the restroom. And the next thing they knew, she was gone. She never returned."

Mia straightened. "Wasn't that around the same time that the supply truck was here?"

Holly blinked. Then she gasped. "Oh, my gosh, you're right."

It all made sense. Lola had been the most negative of people she'd met at dinner, last night. She'd seemed unhappy and bitter. Maybe she'd made a plan to escape, using the supply truck. Maybe that's what all of the girls who'd disappeared had done.

And maybe Lola had had enough.

The only thing was . . . had she escaped? Or had she wound up like Rachel, Carrie, and Madison, burned and abandoned in the middle of the desert?

She glanced back at Todd's tent. He came out of it, red-faced, angry, but also slightly confused by the commotion.

A thought occurred to her. If Todd was here, then he likely had nothing to do with Lola's disappearance. So did that mean he knew nothing about the others? Was she wrong about him?

Behind Mia, a strange hush fell over the crowd, and it started to part. Mia whirled to see Brent, stalking toward them, kicking up a cloud of dust as he moved. Paul was on his heels, along with a couple of other men. "What is this? What's going on?"

"Lola is missing, Brother Brent," a woman said, bowing in reverence.

"Missing?" He looked over at Paul.

"She hasn't been seen since the supply truck left," another person pointed out.

He let out a low curse and went to the gate. Sure enough, people tripped over one another to get out of his way. He stared out past the fence, at the desert, for at least a minute, not speaking. Then he whirled. "Have we gotten in touch with the supply truck driver?"

Paul nodded. "We're attempting to send a message. No word yet."

"Stay on it," he barked, stalking toward the storeroom. "Who the hell let this happen? Jamie? Was it you?"

An older woman, standing in front of the storeroom, whimpered. "No. I promise, it wasn't. She was only gone a short--"

Before she could finish, he reached up and back-handed her across the face. The sound was sharp, like the crack of a whip. She instantly collapsed to the ground, and lay there, sobbing, her body heaving.

Mia let out a gasp, but she was the only one. Everyone else? They were completely still. Almost as if they'd expected it.

Oh, my God, Mia thought, her body trembling. *I need to get out of here.*

But could she? Because though the community said people could leave at any time, she got the feeling these women were being intimidated to stay. Forced into marriages for protection and security. Security from themselves.

Brent walked toward the office and snarled, "Paul. Put more men on the gate for the rest of the week. No one gets in or out. And the second you get in touch with that driver, let me speak to him. Back to work, everyone!"

The crowd instantly began to disperse.

"Brother Brent!" a voice called from behind her.

She knew that voice. It was Todd.

Oh, no.

Brent stopped in his tracks and turned, as did everyone in the area.

Glaring at Mia, he jumped from his tent platform and lumbered toward his leader, as fast as his large body would allow. "I think I have a good idea what happened to her."

Brent crossed his arms. "You do? Then out with it, Brother Todd."

"She was helped to escape." Todd pointed an accusing finger, right at Mia. "By her. That woman is a traitor."

CHAPTER TWENTY FOUR

A collective gasp rose up from the crowd. No one moved.

Mia looked around, and of course, all eyes were on her. Holly whispered, "Oh, no. Is it true?"

She started to deny it, but then Brent said, "What makes you say that, Brother Todd?"

"Because she threatened me with a knife. I was just minding my own business, and she cornered me in my tent and told me she'd kill me. She accused me of doing vile things to Sister Rachel."

More gasps. Brent's eyes fastened on her. "Is this true, Sister Danielle?"

Calm down, Mia. Right now, it's just your word against his. Though she doubted anyone would believe her over an original, it was the only hope she had left. She pressed her sweat slickened hands to her sides and said, "No. I don't know where he's—"

"I saw her!" Someone shouted from the crowd. "I saw her come out of his tent! She was holding a knife!"

That's not good.

She started to back away, but she tripped over someone's feet. She looked over her shoulder to see the accusing eyes of one of the women, staring at her. Everywhere she turned, someone was glaring at her. They seemed to be advancing on her, closing in.

"This is ridiculous," she said, holding up her hands. "It's not true. I—"

"There's the knife!" Someone shouted. "Over there! I see it!"

One of the men ran to the side of Todd's tent and picked it up, out of the dirt. He held it for everyone to see.

Now, the eyes swung back to her, horror and indignation fiercer than ever.

"Killer!" someone shouted.

"Traitor!" another one said.

She gnashed her teeth, looking for escape. She knew what happened in situations like this. Mob justice. Soon, they'd all cast stones at her, and she'd never escape.

But surprisingly, it was Brent who calmed the crowd. "Hold on, people. Hold on! Enough!"

She swallowed. She'd just seen him smack the daylights out of a woman with his bare hand. As much as she wanted to believe he'd be merciful, she didn't trust him. She didn't trust any of them.

He slowly approached her. "Sister Danielle, what do you have to say to this?"

She straightened. "It's not true. Obviously. He's only saying it because he wanted to make me his wife, and I would rather not."

More gasps. Todd snarled, "Why, you lying piece of—"

Brent held up a hand to the man, but his eyes never left Mia's. "Now, Brother Todd. Let's not get too hasty. Why, Sister Danielle, do you think you are in a position to turn down his generous offer of matrimony? Brother Todd is a great man. A respected man in our community. Do you not see that you are not? That you are all alone here?"

"I thought we were a family. I thought we were all equal."

He chuckled. "We are. *If* you follow the rules. If you do, life is much easier for you. If you don't . . ." His smile widened. "It can be very, *very* hard. I promise you; you would not like to find out what happens to the people who disobey us."

Something inside her churned. It was all show, everything he said about being free to do what they wanted, or leave at any time. No, people who came through those gates were captive. "They get to leave. Don't they?" she challenged, just to put him on the spot.

His smile didn't break. "Not always. Not if they make a mockery out of who we are and what we stand for. That threatens our way of life. It threatens *us*. My job is to protect this family. Do you know what happens when people like you challenge our ways? Chaos. And as leader of this community, it's my job to see that there's order, to keep everyone here safe. Do you understand?"

She didn't speak.

"With Lola's leaving, that's already put us on edge. We can't have that continue, you see. If there's a cancer, a rotten apple, you know what needs to be done," he said. "We can't be cavalier about these things and take the easy way out, because there is a chance that it will come back."

She let out an uneasy breath. She could feel the eyes of every member of the community, boring into her. Sweat trickled down her ribcage. Her heart thudded so fast that it hummed in her chest.

"Now," he said in a calm, benevolent voice. "What I think you need to do is go to Brother Todd, apologize, and beg him to take you back. Tell him you are sorry for misbehaving and promise him that it will never happen again. And pray that he will be merciful enough to forgive your transgressions."

She stared at him, the sweat slipping into her eyes now, blurring her sight of him. She could think of nothing she wanted to do less. In fact, no part of her body would even allow her to do such a thing. It was physically impossible.

"No," she said quietly.

His eyes narrowed. He leaned in. "I'm sorry, what?"

"No." This time, she said it much louder, so loud that it elicited more gasps.

He forced out a breath through his nose, his nostrils flaring, and shook his head incredulously. "That's a mistake, Danielle. You leave me no choice but to—"

"Lola?" a voice suddenly said, from near the mess hall tent. "Lola, is that you?"

Everyone turned. It was Holly, standing and pointing away from the front gate.

"I swear I saw Lola, over there!" she insisted. "Behind the office."

One by one, everyone started to turn their attention there. "Are you sure?" someone said.

"Of course I'm sure!" Holly said, heading that way. Soon, several people did the same, and Mia was momentarily forgotten.

It was her chance. She backed away slowly, taking advantage of the distraction. Then, when she was far enough away, she turned and broke into a run, heading for the gate.

Brent, of course, was the first one who noticed that she'd started to run. Before she could even take two steps, he reached out and grabbed hold of her by the hair, yanking her back. "Where do you think you're—"

Before he could finish, she swung around, then jammed her knee squarely into his crotch.

He doubled over, sputtering. "Bitch!" he gasped out, then, as she raced off, screamed, "Idiots! Get her, she's running away!"

Mia set her sights on the gate and rushed toward it, everything else a blur around her. She could hear the pounding footsteps of the men behind her, drawing closer, the shouts and screams of the hysterical women. But as she approached the gate, she realized something.

The padlock was secured, the thick chain wrapped around it.

She wouldn't have time to climb before they were upon her. So she swerved off at a right angle, heading for the tents, looking desperately for somewhere to hide. But in the bright light of midday, there was no place safe enough. Frantic, she scanned the area, the tents. She could hide in one of them, but for how long? And what if they were already occupied?

So she ran on, hiding in the shadows between the tents, crouched low so she took up as little space as possible. When she reached one of the larger tents on a platform, she noticed that there was a small hole there, maybe for a burrowing animal.

Before she could think of what animal it might be, and whether it could be dangerous, someone shouted behind her, spurring her to action. She dove for the hole, landing flat on her stomach and wriggling underneath the platform. In there, it was dark, and the dust coated her nostrils and throat, making her want to cough.

But she held it in. She was hidden. For how long, she didn't know. There, pressed flat against the ground, she waited and watched the feet of the other commune members as they raced back and forth, searching for her. She heard people shouting, Brent screaming in anger, possibly losing even more of his mind. But nobody stopped. Nobody even thought to stoop down and check in her hiding place, and gradually, as it grew darker, Mia's racing heartbeat returned to normal.

There, she made a plan. She would wait until night, until everyone was asleep, and try to make her escape.

*

Lying still, trying not to choke or sneeze on the dust, Mia was thankful not to be in the direct sunlight. Even so, it was oppressively hot, without a breeze. It was only when the sun began to fade that she got some relief, but it was short-lived. The position she was in, lying motionless on her stomach on the hard ground, was excruciating. She deluded herself with thoughts of home, like that surprise birthday party she had when she turned thirty, where her older sister Francine had packed about fifty of her best friends into her tiny downtown Dallas apartment. Mia had cluelessly thought it was simply a sisters' night out, despite Francine's many hints while they were sitting at the center island of the kitchen, drinking wine. They'd all somehow stayed hidden for a full half-hour, until toddler Kelsey started to cry from the bathroom.

She found herself smiling, when suddenly she felt the soft, furry tail of a creature, brushing up against her thigh. Then she heard the sound of something rummaging around in the dirt, near her hip. *Lovely.* Absolutely the last thing she needed right now, to be sharing space with a hungry animal.

But darkness had settled, and voices and sounds had faded off. It was time to go.

Carefully, she crawled forward on her forearms, wiggling out of the tight spot, stopping every so often to make sure no one was near. When she'd pulled herself our far enough to look around, she scanned up and down the row behind the tents. She was alone.

The enclosure was mere yards from her spot. She crept over to it, scanning the area to make sure none of Brent's guards were watching. Then she grabbed ahold of the fence and scaled it, easily. When she threw her leg over the side of it, she looked back for a moment. There were guards stationed at the front gate, but they were facing away from her.

She easily slipped over the fence and landed on the other side.

But she didn't feel free, just yet. She thought of Rachel and the others, women who'd likely tried to escape, and never made it. She'd been out in the desert before, after she first escaped from police custody. She knew how cold it could get, how unforgiving the desert could be. And here, she had no shoes and barely any clothing. She had to find shelter, and quick.

But as she scanned the darkness around her, she doubted she would.

Keeping her head down, she rushed off into the desert, ignoring the jagged rocks and thorny branches of bushes that tore into her feet and legs like blades. She ran parallel to where she thought the path to the gate ran, afraid of attracting the notice of the guards. When her lungs burned and she could run no more, she looked back. The commune was just a soft spot of light in the distance.

It was colder, now, and would only get worse. She hugged herself and scanned for the road. If she took that, eventually she'd wind up in Bracketville. But that was miles away, and she was barefoot and already exhausted.

Eventually, she found the path. It was so dark, and so quiet, the only sound the occasional wail of a coyote. Squinting through the inky blackness, she thought she saw a light, up ahead, the town of Bracketville. It was so faint, so far, but it was her only hope.

She concentrated on putting one foot in front of the other. It was all she could do, now.

CHAPTER TWENTY FIVE

Mia was shivering uncontrollably by the time the sun began to appear over the horizon, in front of her. She was on the verge of delirium, exhausted and dehydrated, so frozen she couldn't feel the rest of her body, and certain that it was over, that she wouldn't be able to make it through the night.

But the sight of the sunlight gave her new energy. She'd been dragging her body toward town, but now, she straightened and moved with renewed purpose. She smiled, her teeth still chattering as she passed the sign that said *NOW ENTERING BRACKETVILLE.*

It was early, so there were few cars and people on the road. She held out a trembling thumb to hitch a ride, but the few trucks that passed did not slow down. She didn't have to wonder why. She probably looked like some refugee, with her hair a mess and her dirt-crusted tunic.

JGT-478. She kept cycling the letters and numbers through her mind, making sure she didn't forget them. JGT-478. JGT-478 . . .

The walk through the desert did one thing. It gave Mia a lot of time to think. Her head churned over the possibilities, and by the time she reached the paved roads of the town, she had a good theory.

The killer wasn't Brent, or Paul, or Todd, as despicable as those men were. No, they'd had no idea about the deaths of the women. So by process of elimination, one person seemed to stick out to her. The truck driver. Whoever he was, he had the best opportunity to commit the crime. Perhaps he lured these girls into a sense of false security by promising to give them a way out, and when he had them alone, he killed them.

Which didn't bode well for Lola.

By now, Mia had had a lot of time to think about it, and she'd determined that Holly hadn't seen Lola at all, in the compound. She'd created a diversion to help Mia escape. Why, Mia had no idea. Maybe because as much as she accepted it, she, too, was sick of their treatment of women. That meant, then, that Lola had truly escaped, with the truck driver.

The killer.

That thought made her break into a run, despite the fatigue and burning pain in her limbs and feet. She couldn't go back to the commune to warn the women there. All she knew was that she had to find that supply truck, somehow. The only problem was, she'd seen it. It was a white truck, without any markings whatsoever. The only thing she had was the license plate.

Not that she could call Marcus and ask him to look into the truck, because her burner phone was long gone.

All of the homes she passed were locked up, but she knew the office of motel she'd stayed at would be open, and it was only a short distance into town. She made it there as the sun freed itself from the horizon. It took every ounce of energy she had to pull open the door to the office. Inside, the icy air conditioning was less than welcoming.

"Sue," she gasped out, her voice raspy from dehydration. Her throat felt like she'd been sucking on razor blades.

A sleepy voice said, "What? Just leave forty dollars on—"

"No, Sue. It's me," she said, leaning up against the counter, feeling dizzy, like she might throw up, since the room was spinning and tilting at an angle. Gasping, Mia tried to collect her thoughts. She couldn't remember what fake name she'd given to Sue, and she knew she didn't look herself, so it took a while for the woman to recognize her.

When she did, Sue's eyes went wide. "My God. What happened to you?"

"I need you to help me," she said, going over to the coffee service and looking for a cup. There was no coffee in the pot, but she was able to get herself some water, which she swallowed down, greedily.

By the time she finished, Sue was actually standing at the counter. "I was thinking about you, when I heard the news today," she said, still eyeing her closely. "Because you were the one asking about those murdered girls. They found another one, out in the desert. Just a few hours ago. I thought it could be you."

"Another one?" Mia let out a breath of exasperation. Lola. She was too late. "Where?"

"Where do you think? Out by that Phantom Bridge."

She shook her head. She'd wasted her shot. She'd been so close to the killer, and now, another woman was dead. She crushed the cup in her hand. "I need your help. Listen. This is very important."

"Yeah. Sure. What do you need?"

"I need you to call the police. I want you to tell them that you have reason to believe that the person who killed those girls is the driver of a supply truck with the license plate JGT . . ." Sue was just staring at her, her mouth slightly opened. She went over and grabbed a pen, shoving it over to her. "Write this down. JGT-478."

Sue picked up the pen and wrote the license plate down. When she was done, she stared at it. "But how do you—"

"Please. Just do it for me," she said, as something caught her attention in the picture window outside.

She only saw it for the briefest of moments because it was speeding down the main drag, but she could've sworn it was a large, white vehicle.

Sue froze with her hand on the phone receiver. "But—"

Mia held up a finger as she went to the window, pressing her face against the cool glass so she could see where it went. But it had gone on, out of sight. "I've got to go. Just do it for me."

She limped through the door. The day was just starting to heat up, but the pavement was still cool on her feet. She ran in the direction of the white vehicle, down the street, stopping at every side-street and driveway to try to spot it. But it was impossible. This was the main drag out of town. It was very likely the truck had just kept going, and was already leaving Bracketville. When she reached a gas station, she slowed, and was about to turn around when she saw it.

It was a white van. Not the supply truck.

Now, what could she do? Not only had she not solved the crime she'd come down here to solve, but she was stuck. She had no money. No clothes. No phone. Nothing.

The best thing she could do was turn around and beg Sue—her only friend in the world—for help. And from what she'd seen of Sue so far, she really doubted the woman would give it to her.

Mia let out a sigh, about to turn back to return to the hotel, when she noticed something familiar.

There was a blue Toyota Corolla hatchback, parked at one of the pumps. Her sister, Francine, had a car like that. Francine, who named everything she owned, had nicknamed it Ol' Blue. She'd had it since she'd started working for the Dallas Police Department.

Mia felt a stab of longing in her heart for her sister. She'd been terrible, not getting in touch with her, though she knew Francine was probably worried out of her mind. She didn't want to put Francine through the trouble of having to lie to the Feds.

But of course, that wasn't Francine. There was no way she'd be here, four-hundred miles from Dallas.

Still, Mia kept staring at it, so wistful that she actually imagined a sticker for UT Dallas on the back bumper. UT Dallas had been Francine's favorite place on earth. All she ever did was brag about how awesome the school was.

Mia blinked, to clear it from her vision.

But the sticker stayed.

And then, something incredible happened.

The door to the convenience store opened, and a little woman with a white-blonde ponytail and dark sunglasses stepped out.

Francine?

She took a step closer, not noticing the car speeding between them until its horn blared and the owner shouted at her. At the commotion, the woman at the gas station looked up.

Then she removed her glasses, and her jaw dropped.

"Mia!"

Mia wanted to cry. Instead, she used whatever strength she had left to run into the arms of her sister.

CHAPTER TWENTY SIX

As he stood in the corner of University Coffee, the coffee shop closest to Mia North's neighborhood, U.S. Marshal Kane Wilcox fully recognized that he was at the end of his rope. How much farther would he sink to try to squeeze blood from this stone?

The teenage girl behind the counter popped her gum and said, "Yeah, of course I know Mia North. I've been serving her ever since I started this job! She was here most mornings and gives great tips."

"Gives?"

"Well, *gave*."

He frowned. Every single person he'd talked to—from the guy who did her dry cleaning to the landscaper who'd done the flowers in the front of their house— was the same. *Mia North is the nicest person. She's really helpful and friendly and amazing. I have nothing bad to say about her.* "So you haven't seen her around lately?"

She shook her head. "Nope. None of us have. It's like she's just disappeared."

He crossed University Coffee off his list and closed his notepad. "Thanks for the information."

Another teenage boy with acne, who'd been watching the conversation, handed him his coffee. "Are you really still trying to find her? Why?"

Wilcox didn't answer, but the girl filled in: "She's a wanted fugitive. Duh. She escaped from prison." Then she wrinkled her nose. "I still can't believe that she did that."

The other kid nodded. "Total badass."

"But really, I don't think she killed that guy. Not her. She's too good. She wouldn't have murdered that man in cold blood, like the news media says."

The boy said, "Well you know, it's all fake news. I think one day we're going to learn it's all a big government conspiracy. You know, like those aliens that are supposed to be running the world? What do you have to say about that, Agent?"

They both stared at him, entirely serious.

Without another word, he turned and left. He was wasting his time.

When he got into his car, he sat there, sipping his coffee, not caring that it burned his tongue. Then banged the heel of his hand on the steering wheel of his car.

He usually got feelings, whenever he was close to pinning his quarry. An itch, in the back of his head, telling him that he was on the right track.

But right now? He felt nothing.

As he drove through University Park, Mia North's hometown, he was at a loss. This was the place she was closest to. Where she lived and grew up, where everyone she was close to resided. Something here should've given him that feeling.

And yet, he hadn't felt this far from nabbing Mia North in weeks. He felt like he was spinning off the wrong track, heading for a cliff.

The partner, David Hunter, had landed him nowhere, which was a disappointment. Days ago, he'd thought for sure that Hunter had something to do with it. That he was feeding her information. But Hunter had been on leave for the better part of a week, and though he'd put surveillance on his house, he hadn't so much as made a single phone call to an unlisted number. All he'd been doing was shuttling his kid to and from school and baseball games.

So he'd shifted his attention to Shields, the tech guy, to see if he could give him any answers. That had been worthless, too.

He knew the drill. He'd tracked down hundreds of fugitives. Usually, everything he learned, as he narrowed in on his target, only served to confirm what a rotten POS the target was.

But with Mia North? It was different. The closer he got, the more it seemed like there was no way in hell she could've done this terrible thing, and the more questions he had. But when he asked those questions? It was like everyone at headquarters didn't have answers. They didn't want to look at it or consider there'd been a mistake. As far as they were all concerned, Mia was their girl, and that was the end.

He couldn't quite explain it, but he felt like he was being pulled along. It brought to mind an old Tennyson quote from his college days. *Yours is not to reason why . . .*

And he was trying not to. He really was. And yet . . .

He'd never felt so doubtful, in all of his years on the force.

Maybe it was his age. Maybe this was proof he was getting softer, and needed to call it quits. Retirement had been calling to him. Maybe it was time to answer that call, go home and finally get to work on all those neglected odd jobs around the house. His wife would be happy.

He found himself clenching his jaw, something that his wife, Dana, would have told him wasn't good for his high blood pressure. He needed to do what she always advised him to do . . . step back, and take a deep breath.

So he pulled to the side of the road, to a small park with a tiny pond. There was a water fountain in the center of it, and a few kids fishing, but other than that, it was deserted. He grabbed his coffee and his Sudoku book and went to a bench to relax.

He sat there for a few moments, finishing his coffee and trying to work out a particularly difficult puzzle. But his mind kept drifting back to Mia. Why hadn't she been in touch with any of the people she knew? Before, he'd been so sure she'd stuck around. And those last two cases, the Jerry Andrews case and the case with the creepy teacher? They'd only intensified the itch at the back of his head. Now, though, he felt like she'd moved on. Maybe she'd finally had enough of this cat-and-mouse and decided to cross the border to Mexico.

Mexico.

There was something about it that Wilcox had found during his digging, that he'd meant to come back to, eventually. And he hadn't. What was it? It was something with the tech guy.

He sat there, pen in hand, staring out at the pond, until it finally hit him.

Right. Marcus Shields. During surveillance, he'd noticed that Mia North's former tech guy had made an awful lot of calls to his sister, Emily Loring, in the past few days. It had seemed odd to him, considering he had records for the past year, and Shields had only been in touch with her a handful of times. It felt like some family drama. Emily Loring had left one voicemail message for him, months ago, and it had sounded suspicious. *Listen. We think she's in Mexico. Bob might go down there to look around.*

He'd meant to look into it, and now was his chance.

He grabbed his phone and typed in: *Emily Loring TX.*

The first result that came back was one that raised his eyebrows:

Remains of Missing Teenager Found Near Phantom Bridge.

He clicked on it.

Police have identified the remains found on the ground of Phantom Bridge as those of Rachel Loring, the 18-year old Waco girl who had been missing since January.

He scanned the rest of the article and determined that Rachel Loring's mother was one Emily Loring. Marcus Shields's sister?

Now, that was interesting. So the murdered girl was Marcus Shields's niece.

Very interesting.

He shifted forward on the bench, trying to glean more information from the article. It turned out that Rachel Loring was one of three young women who'd disappeared from their homes, presumed to have run away, only for their remains to be found months later, burned, in this remote desert area of Southwest Texas.

Agent Wilcox didn't know Mia North well, but from what he did know about her, this sounded like a case that would be right up her alley.

And what if Marcus Shields, being an expert tech guy, had lied to him? What if he'd caught wind of some of her communication, and blackmailed her into looking into this case for him? Now, that was an interesting thought. It might be a leap, but he'd heard of stranger things in his career.

At this point, he was running out of things to go on. This seemed like as good a lead as any. He closed his Sudoku book, tossed his empty cup in the trash, and hurried to his car. Maybe it was time for a little drive out into the desert.

CHAPTER TWENTY SEVEN

Mia was finally starting to feel human again.

It started with a shower at the hotel room Francine had rented at Sue's place. Then, though Francine had always been the taller one, she'd loaned Mia some of her clothes. Now, they sat at the table in the hotel room, eating what Mia thought was the best burger she'd ever had, even though it just came from Jack in the Box, and talking about the case.

Well, sometimes. Most times, they just gushed at how good it was to see each other again. Francine reached over and grabbed her hand. "Mom and Dad miss you so much. I have to call them and tell them you're okay."

"You know you can't," she said, shaking her head. "I have this crazy U.S. Marshal after me, and I think he's surveilling everyone I know. Maybe even you."

"I don't think he is. He asked me questions in the beginning, but he never came back. Because I think I passed the test, since I really didn't know where you were." She munched on a French fry. "I can't believe you came out here for this case! You have so much going on. Aiden, Kelsey, they need you. We need to get you back home."

"Look, I am working on that, but as far as this case, I had no choice. But I think, even if Shields hadn't pushed the case on me, I'd have wanted to come out, anyway. The more I look into this case, the weirder it gets."

"I can see that," Francine said, looking over the details of the case Mia had brought up on her laptop. "All three of these girls were set on fire and burned in the desert?"

She nodded. "Yep. And the latest one was Lola. From the commune. Of course, they don't know that it's her, yet, but I'm sure it is. She escaped right before."

Francine listened her nodding. "Wow. So tell me about this place. Was it really like the Stone Ages, with cavemen dragging women around by their hair and everything?"

"Yep. Even worse. They were polygamists. But the worst thing was that they all acted like it was perfectly normal. Even the women were fine with being treated like second-class citizens. Well, most of them." She shuddered at the memory of how happy some of them were. "And the thing was, they kept saying that anyone could leave at any time. But they locked up the gates, for safety, they said. And when Lola did run off, there was chaos. It was like a prison for them. I'm sure of it."

She took a long slurp of her soda, her throat getting dry at the thought of that long, painful walk through the desert.

"Wow. So what do you think happened?"

"It's like I told you. I think she arranged with that truck driver for him to take her out. And he killed her. The people in the commune didn't even know these girls were dying once they escaped. That's how cut off from everything they are."

"Well," she said, tapping on her laptop. "Like I said, I'm tracing that license plate."

"I don't know if that's a good idea. What if Gavin—"

"It's Gavin," she rolled her eyes. "You know Gavin. He loves me."

That much was true. Francine had always had her share of admirers, and Gavin, one of the officers in her precinct, had been number one. They'd dated once, about a thousand years ago, and he still carried a torch, sending her flowers and pledging his love at every turn. But Francine was a free spirit and had never found anyone she wanted to settle down with. Mia had always called her too picky.

"I hope you're right."

"Please. I know I am," she said, checking her phone. "Oooh. He's gotten back to me. He says the truck is registered to a business right here in Bracketville. Southwest Market, on Broad Street." She typed something into her phone. "That's only a few blocks from here."

"Perfect." Mia stood up. "Let's go."

They grabbed their things and got into Ol' Blue. Francine drove them around the block, to a busy supermarket. Sure enough, when they pulled into the back lot, they noticed a number of white trucks parked there. It was easy to pick out the one that Mia had seen, even without the license plate—it was the only one covered in desert dust. It was parked at the end of the fleet. Mia's heart jumped in her throat. "There! There it is."

"All right, all right," Francine said, pulling into the first open parking space. "You stay here. I'll go in and ask who was driving it."

Francine jumped out even before Mia could protest. That was her sister. As much as Mia liked to take the bull by the horns, Francine always wanted to be first, with everything. And she loved doing this kind of thing, researching cases. That's why the officers at her precinct loved her.

Mia watched her saunter toward the back entrance of the market. As usual, men turned their heads to watch her. She managed to flag down an older gentleman who seemed more than happy to help. She pointed out the truck, and he nodded. They spoke for a few moments, and she smiled, thanked him, and turned to Mia with a big grin and a double thumbs-up.

"Bingo!" she said when she climbed in Ol' Blue and started the engine. "He said that truck is driven out only on supply runs once a week, by Jorge Hernandez. The best thing is that he's inside right now, and is just about to leave for lunch."

She started to pull out, and Mia said, "Wait, where are we going?"

"Well, I told the guy that I was his girlfriend and wanted to surprise him by taking him out to lunch," she said sheepishly, lurching out of the spot.

"What? Why did you—"

"It was the only way I could find out if he was in there! They'd be suspicious if I said I was some cop, wanting to ask him questions about some girls he might have killed."

"I guess that's good thinking," Mia said.

She pulled into a spot to the side of the market, but still in viewing distance of the truck. "Of course it is. Look," she motioned through the windshield. Sure enough, there was a man, wearing a red baseball cap, walking toward the truck. "Is that him?"

She vaguely recalled seeing the truck pulling in, before she'd gone into the tent with Todd. "I think so. Let's follow him."

"My specialty!" she cooed with glee, shifting into reverse.

Mia wasn't exactly sure when tailing a suspect had become her sister's specialty, since most of her work for the Dallas Police had been behind a desk. But she didn't question it. She was glad to have a partner again, one she knew she could absolutely trust. She pointed through the windshield. "He's making a left turn over on Military Ave—"

"I got it, I got it," Francine said, pulling out of the lot and crossing three lanes of traffic to the middle turning lane. She caught the light green at the last second and made the turn, a few car lengths behind the truck.

"Now, you don't want to get too close—"

"I got it," she argued, rolling her eyes. "Didn't I tell you, this was my specialty? What, you don't believe me?"

"Well, I didn't—"

"Just because you're a fancy Fed and I'm not, doesn't mean I don't know a thing or two."

It had long been a bone of contention in their family—her dad, a Dallas Police Officer all his life, had been so proud when Mia had gotten her ticket to the show in Quantico. But Francine had always teased her that she was "too good for us locals." Francine always teased, though. That was just their relationship. Mia knew she'd been just as proud of her little sister.

And it turned out that Mia didn't have to be a backseat driver. Francine did know a thing or two. Though she'd never be great with a firearm, and she'd much rather hand out tickets than do anything that got her hands dirty, Francine tailed the truck perfectly. They followed it into a parking lot for a Subway sandwich shop, which was nearly empty after the main lunch rush.

Mia pulled off her seatbelt, ready to pounce.

Francine pulled into a parking space across from him and said, "What's our plan, here?"

She already had the door open. She glanced back. "What do you mean? I'm going to ask him questions."

"You want me to be your back-up?"

"I can handle it. Just wait here."

"Wait, wait, wait! I can handle the hard stuff, too, Mia. I'm not just a desk girl. You saw how I worked with the guy at the supermarket. I can—"

"I know," she said, "But—"

"But nothing. I'm tired of everyone thinking I can't handle myself, just because I'm blonde and pretty. I can do—"

"You don't like to fire a gun."

"Yes, right! Because I always break my nails. But that doesn't mean I don't like to—"

"Look. We can argue about this later. He's getting out."

She jumped out of Ol' Blue and rushed to his truck, just as he was getting out of it. "Excuse me!" she said politely. "George Hernandez? Can I ask you a few questions?"

He slammed the door to his truck and grunted. "Jorge." He looked her over. "What do you want? Who are you?"

It was only when she was standing right beside him that she realized how large he was. He was easily six-five, and solid, towering over her, with tattoos up and down his muscled arms. He had a menacing look to him, fists clenched, breathing hard through his nostrils, like he wanted to clobber her.

"Sorry. Jorge. I just have a question about a friend. She was coming from that commune you delivered to yesterday. I was told she was supposed to get a ride with you, but she never arrived."

He suddenly looked nervous. "I don't know nothing about no commune."

"The Rising Sun? The man at the supermarket said you do. That you drive there, out into the desert, once a week to deliver supplies. You did it yesterday, which is why your truck is all covered in dust."

He shrugged. "All right. Yeah. I went out there. I didn't know it was a commune. Thought it was a camp, or something. What's it to you? I don't know nothing about no girl."

She eyed him suspiciously, not sure if she believed him. "Then you don't care that you were the last person to see her alive? She was found murdered, hours after she hitched a ride into the desert. Since you're the only truck that went through, she has to have hitched that ride with you."

His eyes widened. "Who the hell are you?"

"Someone who can make your life really miserable, really quickly."

He scoffed. "You're kidding me, right?"

He tried to move off, but she placed both hands on the center of his chest and shoved him, hard. "Nope."

He backed off, surprised. "Look, I just want to get a sandwich. What do you want from me?"

"You can get that sandwich. All you gotta do is tell me. Did you take that girl from the commune?"

Jorge sighed. "All right. Yeah. I did. Sometimes I transport girls from there. A woman gives me a couple hundred dollars to take them out and then drop them in the middle of the desert. It's easy cash for me. That's all."

"A woman? Who?"

He shrugged. "I don't know her name. She's older. That's it."

"What does she look like?"

Jorge let out a laugh. "I don't know. Old bag. I only saw her once. Years ago. Since then, she leaves the money with the money for the supplies. So I never see her anymore. I just stop when I get about a mile out of the compound, and if there's a girl inside, she gets out. But I don't even see them. So yeah, I think there was a girl yesterday." He swallowed, and his eyes flooded with sympathy. "You say she's dead?"

Mia didn't answer. She was busy thinking about her next move. It pained her, but she knew what she had to do.

"If she's dead, I ain't got nothin' to do with it. I promise."

Mia scowled at him. "You might not have killed them, but you left the girls in the middle of the desert and drove away. You didn't try to help them. You didn't even look back!"

"Look. I didn't want to get involved. I knew something weird was goin' on, but I got a family to feed. I can't get myself tangled up in—"

"And I guess you heard about all these murdered girls, found in the desert, and just convinced yourself it had nothing to do with your deliveries?" she accused.

"Yeah," he shrugged. "I wanted to believe it had nothing to do with those girls. Yeah."

Of course. She knew his type. Too many people these days were so jaded that they wanted to bury their heads in the sand and say, *Not my problem.*

Even though she'd seen a lot of bad in this world, she'd always been determined never to be like that. "When are you going back there?"

"Not until next week."

That wasn't good enough. "No. You're going back sooner."

He squinted at her. "But I can't—"

"Make an excuse. Tell them you forgot to deliver something. I don't care what it is. You're going back there tonight."

"Tonight? But—"

"Don't screw with me, Jorge. Get in touch with your contact there and tell them you're on your way. Can you?"

He looked away, relenting. "Fine. Yeah. I can."

"All right," she said, removing her hands from his chest. "Here's what's going to happen. Go in and get your sandwich. Then, we're going to go back to the store and pack an extra crate of supplies that you 'forgot' to drop off to them. I don't care what it is. You understand?"

He sighed. "Yeah, I guess I can. I forgot a crate of yeast the last time I was there. I told them I'd bring it next week. I guess I can tell them I'll bring it over early, out of the goodness of my heart."

"Good. Do that. When you go, though, I'll be hiding in the back of your truck."

He stared at her, confused. "What? What are you going to do?"

"It's no business of yours. You just drive there and do exactly what you normally do. Stop where you normally stop. I don't want you do to a single thing differently. All right?"

He nodded.

She let him go, and he hurried into the sub shop. Meanwhile, she returned to Ol' Blue, where Francine was watching intently through the driver's side window. "Hey, Rambo," she said, even before Mia had opened the door. "You think you might want to take it easy?"

"Why?"

"Um, Mia. That guy was huge! You really shoved him! He could've clobbered you. That's why you need me. I have a softer touch, Mia, and I can--"

Mia waved her sister away. "It's fine. He told me what I needed to know—that some older woman arranged passage for the women on the truck, from inside the compound."

"A woman? Who?"

"I don't know. But he's going to help us find out."

She gave her an incredulous look. "He is? How? He didn't really look like he was in a helpful mood, after he met you."

"I don't really care what kind of mood he's in. I'm going back to the commune, in his truck," she explained. "And I need you to stay back at the drop-off point and stake it out."

"You're going back?" her sister asked, horrified.

"Yes."

"Well, if you're going, I'm going, too. I'm not going to let you go in there while I'm eating coffee and donuts. It's totally—"

"I need you to stay outside. You need to be there, in case I don't return."

Her eyes widened. "Mia, you really think you might not? Why do you want to risk it?"

Mia shrugged. "If I had a better idea, believe me, I'd go for it. The last place I want to be is back there. But I think it's the only way we'll find out what the hell is going on."

CHAPTER TWENTY EIGHT

Mia huddled under some sacks in the back of the white truck as it bumped on the dusty road toward the compound.

As she sat there, she thought about the other women who'd come before her. Had they sat in this exact spot, hoping to find freedom? Who had they arranged their escape with?

She thought about the older women she'd met, Barbie and Charlie, and the many others she'd seen around the commune. Had one of them really arranged for these women to be removed from the commune? Were they in cahoots with someone outside of the commune who'd kill them? For what reason?

It was getting towards evening. Thanks to a long nap at the hotel room, she was rested. After about twenty minutes of hiding there, she heard the brakes screech, the truck idling under her. After a moment, she heard Jorge shout out, "Got that extra shipment of yeast you need. I told Paul I was coming."

She heard a man say, "All right, all right. One second."

There was a metallic sound of the gates creaking open, and the truck began to rumble up the road again.

This was it. She sucked in a breath as the truck came to a stop. Then, a moment later, the door in the back of the truck opened, casting her in the dying light of day. She scrunched her body down and low peered at him from under a sack. His gaze swept over her as he grabbed the carton of yeast from the bed of the truck and carried it off.

It was time.

Just as she was about to rise from her hiding spot and climb out, another form appeared at the back of the truck, silhouetted in light. It wasn't Jorge. One look at the shape, and she knew it was a woman. The woman crawled into the back of the truck quietly, and sunk down among the empty sacks breathing hard and trembling.

Another escapee?

This wasn't expected. Her plan had been to poke around the compound and see if she could find the old woman who'd arranged it.

But now, an even better plan formed in her mind. If there was a pick-up arranged for today, then she needed to be there for it.

Before she could get a good look at the woman, the door of the truck slammed closed, casting them in darkness. A moment later, the engine started up again, and the truck began to rumble off.

She sat there, absolutely still, listening to the woman's frightened breathing for a few minutes, and wondering what she should do. She decided to remain quiet, so as not to scare the girl anymore. By then, the truck had left the compound.

Sure enough, when the truck stopped again, the woman jumped up and pushed open the back of the truck, then slipped out. Mia watched her step into the light for a brief moment before disappearing out of sight.

It was Holly.

Mia rose to her feet, went to the end of the container, and jumped from the truck, just as it resumed its trip. She landed on the hard ground and looked around as the truck headed off into the distance, expecting to see her sister, right where they'd left her.

But she didn't see Francine anywhere.

All she saw was Holly, standing there, looking confused. "Sister Danielle?" she asked when the dust around them settled. "What are you doing here? I thought you were dead! That's what they said. That you ran and you probably--"

"No. Now listen to me. What was the plan, here? Were you planning to meet someone?"

She nodded. "I was trying to escape. After what happened to you, I'd had enough. So I was told that all I needed to do is get into the truck, get off when it stopped, and a man would be waiting to take me to the nearest town. But . . . there's no one here."

"Yes," she said, looking around for Francine. That was really odd. Cupping her hands around her mouth, she called, "Francine!"

She'd hoped her sister would poke her head out from one of the giant boulders in the area, but she didn't.

"Who's Francine?" Holly asked, hugging herself. "I was supposed to meet a man. What's going on here?"

Mia wished she could answer that. It didn't make any sense. They'd dropped Francine here, before, and Mia had told her to stay hidden and stake it out, to see if the mysterious man arrived. Had she?

It wasn't like Francine to give up and go home. If anything, Francine would've offered to do more. When they'd dropped Francine off, she'd once again complained that she wished she could've gone with her.

With a sinking feeling, it hit Mia.

What if the man had come early, and Francine had given herself up to him, pretending to be his pick-up?

Her heart jumped into her throat as she looked around, frantic, for her sister.

"Francine!" she shouted, as loud as she could. But the word echoed across the vast desert. She was nowhere in sight.

CHAPTER TWENTY NINE

This was a mistake.

Francine Clopecki knew that, the second she started to follow the man into the desert.

It had been a split-second decision. A stupid, rash one, too. As proud as she'd been about her little sister Mia getting into the FBI, she had to admit, it had always been hard, watching the family attention fall on her. *Oh, what case are you working on, Mia? Where are you going this time, Mia? Wow, Mia, your work is always so exciting!* That was pretty much how family get-togethers went. Her father had been proud to see Francine follow him into the Dallas PD, but he knew the precinct where she worked, and he knew that the most she'd ever had to handle were search warrants and unpaid traffic tickets. It had never been as exciting as anything Mia had done.

Not that she'd ever put herself out there. Most people looked at her and thought she was too pretty to be a cop. That's what Gavin always said to her. And she'd been fine with it. She considered it her secret weapon—her looks got her places.

But now, she was nearly forty. And she wasn't nearly as pretty as she had been. Call it a mid-life crisis. One morning, she'd woken up and realize that she'd hardly done anything important in her life. She didn't have family, she didn't have any major cases she'd solved; she was a mediocre police officer in a suburban town.

And so, when David Hunter had gotten in touch with Francine and told her that there was a way she could help, she'd jumped at it. She'd relished working with Mia, tracking down a killer. It was all so exciting.

Now, though, she got the feeling she'd taken it too far.

She'd just been sitting there, waiting for the man to arrive, thinking that Mia was going to get all the glory for solving this case yet *again*, and she was going to be on the sidelines. Not that Mia could get the glory, since she was on the run. But somehow, she was sure that her part in this case would amount to very little.

She'd been so deep in thought about that, that she hadn't even noticed him arrive.

He'd sneaked up on her. Tall, handsome, like one of those cowboys on Yellowstone, he didn't look anything like a killer. He was too normal, maybe a bit rugged, with a bit of stubble on his chin, but other than that, very vanilla. Wasn't that the way all killers looked? *He was so normal, quiet, kept to himself*. . .

He'd looked her over, confusion and desire in his eyes. She was used to the desire—most men eyed her that way. But the confusion, she understood, too—she'd seen how Mia looked after escaping that place, and assumed most women he ran across looked just as rough around the edges. He probably hadn't expected one with so much mascara and hair product.

Once she'd gotten over the surprise, she'd smiled at him. Mia always used the rough tack, but Francine held to the adage about catching more flies with honey. "Hey, there," she'd said, "You scared me."

He'd looked her over, his dark eyebrows tenting. "You're the girl I'm supposed to be picking up?"

And then she'd said the words she was now deeply regretting. "Sure am. That's me! Ready to go! Where we off to?"

Now, as they walked off into the middle of the desert, she couldn't help thinking she'd made a massive mistake. At first, he'd been curious as to why she was dressed so well, and she'd attempted to flirt with him, to keep things light.

But gradually, he'd been talking less and less. Now, he was completely silent. She kept babbling stupidly, hoping to open him up, but it wasn't working. And she had a gift, at least, she thought. She could get anyone to talk about anything. Usually even shy people opened up around her. But this guy had become a closed book.

As she walked, she brushed the butt of her service revolver at her hip.

She hadn't used it since she graduated from the academy, but if she needed it, it was there. Somehow, that didn't really make her feel any better. Mia was the crack-shot. They always joked that Francine couldn't hit the broad side of a mountain if she was standing right in front of it.

In fact, she hadn't even arrested anyone. Usually, she came in for the booking, after the police had done the dirty work. Did she even know how to use the handcuffs she toted around with her? She couldn't be sure.

Francine sucked in a breath, then let it out slowly, trying to calm herself. Finally, when they reached the gentle slope of the mountain she said, "Where are we going?"

He kept walking. No answer.

She stopped. "I'm not exactly wearing the shoes for a hike," she said, pointing to her ballet flats.

He slowed, but did not turn. Instead, he walked sideways, toward a boulder, and reached behind it, pulling out a rumpled paper bag.

She tilted her head, curious. "What's that?"

He didn't answer. Instead, he reached in and pulled out several things. Some rope. A box of matches. Lighter fluid. And, finally, a knife.

Now, she didn't just have a feeling. She *knew* this was a mistake.

Francine took a step back. "What are you doing with all that, honey," she said, her voice still sweet as ever. "You're scaring me."

She hoped he'd say something like it was all a joke, but he didn't. He simply began to unwind the rope. Then he grabbed the knife and stepped toward her.

She fumbled for the gun beneath her jacket. She wished she could've done this with practiced confidence, like Mia could, but her fingers were slick with sweat. Pulling it out, she pointed it at him. It wavered in front of her. "Stop right there. I'm a cop." There was something else she had to say, too, wasn't there? "And . . . you're under arrest."

He didn't stop. Not for one instant. He moved forward, calling her bluff.

She stepped back, once, twice. "I'm serious. I'm going to—"

He reached for her, and she screamed and pulled the trigger. She'd forgotten about the recoil and almost dropped the gun in shock. *I fired my pistol. This is really happening. Oh, my God, this is really happening. I'm dead.* The shot went wide, just as she'd expected. By then, he was upon her, the knife's blade glistening in the last light of day.

CHAPTER THIRTY

The cracking sound of the gunshot was unmistakable. It echoed through the valley, all around her, so that Mia couldn't quite tell where it came from.

She scanned the area in the rapidly descending darkness, and that was when she heard the scream.

It was Francine.

"Stay here," she told Holly, now certain as to where the sound had originated from. There were dark mountains in the distance, and she was pretty sure that was where she needed to head.

She raced as fast as she could, now having little trouble on the terrain, thanks to her sister's sneakers. Francine. Of course, in a lot of ways, she was like Mia. She wanted to help. No matter what the cost.

If anything happened to Francine, she'd never be able to forgive herself. She pumped her legs and arms, willing herself to go faster despite the burning of her lungs. She flew, now, over bushes and ravines, not thinking of anything else but her sister. Everything blurred but her destination.

When she stopped for a moment to collect her bearings and figure out where she was, a bullet whizzed past her ear.

Instinctively, she dove behind some bushes, out of sight, as she heard Francine's high-pitched shriek. As she strained to see between the branches, Francine's captor fired another round, which went wide.

In the darkness, she saw the man, standing, with a gun pressed against Francine's temple. Her sister was standing still, the large man, towering over her from behind. Mia needed to do something, and quick.

"Whoever you are!" she called, breathing hard. "This is the FBI. We know everything. Please, let her go."

There was no response. Mia slowly peered up over the edge of the bushes and gnashed her teeth.

Francine's face looked as white as the moon, but she wasn't trembling, and she didn't look scared. Maybe that was the old Clopecki bravery. Why else would she have elected to come out here, alone with the man, knowing he was a killer? Whatever it was, she seemed strangely accepting of this. The man, however, looked clearly upset. He looked strangely normal, like any father one would find in the pick-up line at school. Middle-aged, with graying hair and a solid build.

The man said, "Go away. Don't try to stop me."

"That's not happening," Mia called out. "I'm not leaving until you hand over the woman."

"I'm going to kill her, no matter what. If you try to stop me, I'll kill you, too," he shouted, voice gravelly, his head pivoting slightly as he searched off into the murky dusk. "So you're better off just turning around and getting the hell out of here."

"Who are you? What do you want?"

He chuckled. "Nothing you can give me."

"And what's that?" she called, trying to sound calm as she surveyed her surroundings, her mind churning. She needed a plan.

"I want to see her burn. I want to hear her squeal as she burns," he hissed to the sky. "I love that sound. The sound of flames crackling mixing with the screams of pain. It's like music to my ears. I'm addicted to it."

Mia's blood went cold. So they were dealing with a homicidal pyromaniac. Strange, he'd looked so normal, so much like the dad next door, she'd been hoping she could reason with him. But with those words, she knew that was impossible.

He'd kill Francine and set her on fire, no matter what she did.

Francine, why did you have to pick right now to use that Clopecki bravery?

It was still hot, even without the sun, bearing down on her. Sweat trickled into her eyes, blurring her vision. She looked up, wiping it from her eyes. The next time she did, she could only see the outline of the man, holding her sister.

Could he see her? It was getting darker by the moment, and the sun had long since gone behind the mountains, casting dark shadows over the valley.

Wanting to test that, she grabbed a couple of rocks and tossed them off to the side.

Sure enough, the man followed the noise. He swung the gun in that direction, squinting to see.

So he didn't know exactly where she was. She could definitely use that to her advantage. Mia looked around, trying to decide how to best use the rapidly descending darkness. She couldn't wait too long. If she did, it would be absolutely black, and then she would be able to see nothing at all.

Crouching below the line of bushes, she frog-walked as quietly as she could, trying to come up behind him. As she started to, Francine seemed to get the hint, because she spoke, "You won't get away with this."

Classic line, spoken only to distract him. Good ol' Francine. She knew exactly what Mia was up to. It was just like when they were kids, and Mia used to have to distract her parents from the fact that Francine was coming home from a date, way past curfew. How many times had they played tricks like that? For them, working as a team was second nature.

He chuckled again. "I think I already have, girl. I've done this plenty of times. I'll never get caught."

"So, what do you do?" Francine asked, sounding remarkably calm despite the gun pressed against her temple. "You work with someone in the commune? Is that it? An old lady? And she promises these girls who are at the end of their rope and want to escape a way out, only to feed them to you?"

By now, Mia was just at the man's side, flat against the ground, using a small bush for cover. It wasn't enough. He could easily see her, if he turned that way. But thank God for Francine. She'd always been able to talk to a wall.

"Yeah. That's about right." He seemed happy with the fact.

"Who is the woman? And how did you meet her?"

The man seemed all too happy to speak about this, as many psychotic killers often did. This was their hobby, and everyone like to talk about their hobbies, if only anyone would be interested. And now that he had a sounding board, he was ready to spill the whole, sordid story.

"It was about nine years ago. I met her in town, in Bracketville. Until then, I'd been working only with Mexican immigrants. They were safe. They come over the border, no one's looking for them. And there were plenty to work with, so I've been doing that since I was a kid. But people talk. The Border Patrol agents knew about it. I was kind of a legend. So I guess she heard of my handiwork, and she was curious because she said there were people she wanted to wipe off the map, because they were making trouble for her people. She was out looking for someone. Someone special. So we made a plan that if they wanted to get rid of someone, she'd put them on a truck and have them get off in the middle of nowhere. And I'd take care of the rest."

Francine's voice was tight. "And her name?"

"Her name's Barbara."

Mia let out a breath. Barbie. She'd been expecting that. The woman had been so intent on preserving their way of life, and admonishing anyone who tried to change it. She wanted to cut these women who were poisoning the rest of the community out, just like a cancer, like Brent had said. But they couldn't allow word of what was going on in the community to get back to the general population. If more people came there and realized what they were up to, it would spell the end of their comfortable way of life.

"Barbara?" Francine said. "And you guys have been working this together for . . . how long? Nine years?"

"That's right. She paid the truck driver not to say anything. That place, they got a slew of problems. Everyone in it is running away from something. And from what I hear, in a lot of cases, it's something really bad." He laughed. "I think it's a perfect racket for them. They get a bunch of stupid people to do their dirty work, and they live like kings . . . instead of where they should be living, which is in prison. No wonder they don't want anyone telling the outside world what they're up to."

"Wow . . . like what things have they done?"

He shrugged. "I don't know. Who knows? The story is that the guy was a wanted man in LA for some shit he did, and so he escaped out to Rising Sun to avoid whatever was after him."

"Ah . . . wow," Francince said again. "Crazy." She hesitated, maybe she was running out of things to say. Mia had to act fast. Now, she was in position. Still crouched, she slowly and quietly crept up behind him.

"Ready to get this party started?" he said.

"Yeah," Mia shouted, lunging for him. She threw herself on his back, her first priority to get the gun out of Francine's way. She grabbed the man's wrist with one hand and the gun with the other, prying it from his fingers, then held tight to the handle of it as she crashed to the ground.

"What the—" he snarled, shocked.

He reached for her, and as he tried to wrench it away from her, backing away, Francine loosened herself from the bear hug he'd had her in and sprang, elbowing him in the throat.

Stunned, the man toppled a little, before falling down on his backside, coughing and choking out, "You bitches! What are you—"

Mia crawled to her feet and leveled the gun at him. "Don't move."

*

Moments later, Francine had the man with his hands cuffed behind his back. "I never actually used these things!" she said in delight as the cuffs snapped shut.

Mia gazed at her incredulously. "You need to get out more."

"True. I've booked plenty of jerks, but I never actually arrested anyone. This would be my first. I like it."

They shoved the man down on a boulder, and Mia said, "Want to tell us who you are and where you're from?"

Avoiding eye contact, the man growled, "You are going to pay for this. Both of you."

They ignored the threats. "Okay, you want to do it the hard way then, huh?" Mia reached into the pocket of the man's shirt and pulled out his wallet. She opened it. "Doug Lancaster from Del Rio, huh?" When the man didn't answer, she paged through his things and held up his driver's license. "This is expired."

He shrugged.

She closed it and shoved it back into his shirt. As she turned, she saw a figure in white, kind of like an apparition, walking up behind her. She almost raised her gun, but then the woman said, "That was some action, Sister Danielle . . . are you a cop?"

"Something like that, Holly," Mia said, taking off her jacket and handing it to the woman, who was shivering. "Are you all right?"

Holly nodded. "Barbie told me she could get me out, and I believed her. She was my friend. My best friend in there."

Mia sighed and touched the woman's arm. "You didn't have any friends in there. Where's home for you? Do you have a family?"

"I'm from Yuma, Arizona. I have a husband. He's a good man. We had a fight and I left. It's stupid, now, to think I came here to escape. I didn't realize how good I had it."

Mia smiled. "You're safe, now. We can make sure you get back home, if that's what you want."

She nodded.

Mia turned to her sister. "Francine, this is what we're going to have to do. We have to find a way back to town, first."

Francine said, "That's not a problem. Doug Lancaster, over here, told me he parked his truck over that ridge. Assuming he's not lying, I can go get it," she said, glaring at their prisoner. She stooped over him, feeling in his pockets, and pulled out a set of car keys. "Well, what do you know?"

"Good. I don't want to walk that again, if I don't have to," Mia said.

Francine smiled. "Well, it sure was fun, being an FBI agent for a day. Even if I almost got myself killed. Who knows, maybe I'll finally send my own application in?"

"Sorry. You have to be under thirty-seven years of age." She smirked. They were big on teasing one another for getting old.

She stuck out her tongue at her sister. "Oh, I'm sure they can make exceptions for me."

"I'm in no position to help you there, sis."

"Damn. That's true." Francine shrugged and looked out toward the commune. "But what do we do next? We're going to have to call the police. And you . . ."

"Right. *You're* going to have to, because I can't. Both of you," she said, looking around. Night had really fallen now, and the moonlight was strong above them, but soon, it wouldn't be safe to travel. "Go and get that truck. Can I use your phone?"

Francine handed it to her. Luckily, it still had a little bit of charge. There was no service, not out here in the desert, but she'd send the message now, and eventually, when they got to town, it would go through.

Luckily, she remembered Marcus Shields's number. She typed in:

Rachel Loring murderer Doug Lancaster being transported to custody. Doug was aided by a woman named Barbara from the Rising Sun Commune. Please send agents to the commune north of Bracketville. Supposedly several wanted criminals there.

Then she placed her phone in the pocket of her jeans, put her arm around Holly, and waited for her sister to arrive with the truck.

CHAPTER THIRTY ONE

What a difference a little preparation made.

With good sneakers, a backpack filled with necessities, and enough money to last her awhile, Mia had hiked into the desert to catch the action from afar. She hid in the foothills, looking down upon the valley and the commune, as the FBI arrived. Right on time.

Sipping ice water from her canteen and wearing plenty of sunblock, she watched as the FBI swarmed the compound, pulling out Barbie and Brent and Paul and the others, instructing them to lay on their stomachs in the dirt as they were cuffed and taken away. Utility vans came to take the other members of the commune away. Apparently, there were whispers of lots of criminal goings-on around the compound, and the psycho serial killer was only scratching the surface.

And she and her sister had brought it all down. Together.

She smiled, already missing Francine. They'd brought Doug to the Bracketville police, and when the message finally went through, Marcus transmitted the message to the proper authorities so that they were all over it. Then, they'd ensured Holly had enough food and clothing, and dropped her off at the bus station with a one-way ticket back to Yuma.

After it was all under control, Francine hugged Mia and headed off, earlier that morning, after piling up her things into Ol' Blue. It made sense that she leave before the place was swarming with law enforcement, because it would only cast suspicion on her. Now, the place definitely was swarming—the FBI had probably been coordinating the raid all night, considering how many agents were involved. It looked like ants, storming a chocolate chip cookie.

They were going to close it down. That much was certain. It was funny to think that in another few hours, once they got done making arrests and collecting evidence, the place would be empty. Forgotten, once again. And then, without the threat of a bunch of misogynist pigs lording over the place, it likely would be a perfect place for someone like Mia to hide out in.

But she knew that as easy as it would be to run away from her troubles, she couldn't do that. She had a family to get back to.

Now, she had to get out, too, before they put two and two together and realized she was a part of this story, as well.

Mia turned from her view above the compound, grabbed her walking stick and started the long hike down the mountain. As she walked, she thought about her sister, and how thankful she was to have her as an ally. If she hadn't come along, Mia would've probably been dead.

She was still smiling when she reached the town of Bracketville, intending to gather the rest of the supplies Francine had arranged for her to have and get out on the road. Before she'd headed back to Dallas, Francine had arranged for her to have an old beater car, filled with gas, as well as a new burner phone.

As Mia arrived in the city limits, she checked her phone. She had a message from a number she didn't recognize. *Thanks for everything. I owe you one.*

She knew who it was, though. Marcus Shields. Maybe, now, her family would feel a sense of peace, knowing what had happened to poor Rachel. She was happy he owed her a favor—in the future, she might need his help.

Now, Mia felt like she had a new lease on life. When she reached the hotel on the outskirts of town, she found the old car—a Chevy Nova from the seventies that was all rust— waiting for her, right outside the room. Curiously, though, another car was parked beside hers, which was strange. Beside Ol' Blue, which was now probably on its way to Dallas, she'd never seen another car in the parking lot. This one was a nice white sedan, from Alamo Rental, according to the sticker on the bumper.

I guess Sue finally rented out a room to someone other than me and the resident drug pusher.

As she went to her room, the door of the room next to her sprang open. A shiver went down her spine, and in her mind, she imagined that U.S. Marshal, finally catching up with her. When the form stepped behind her, she curled her fingers into a fist, ready to let it fly.

Whirling, she wound up to throw that punch, and froze. She let out a gasp.

It was Aiden.

"Oh!" she cried, pulling him into a hug, all the tension in her limbs releasing.

"Shh," he said, nudging her through the open door to her room. When she was in there, already crying from the shock of finally seeing her husband again after so long, he closed the door quietly and added, "I don't have much time. I'm on a business trip. I don't know how she managed it, but Francine arranged it for me. But I need to get driving. I'm expected to be in El Paso by nightfall. I got 'lost.'"

"Oh," she said, disappointed. He was right. The FBI were in town, and that meant it was too dangerous to stay in one place. She had to get moving, soon, too. "But can't we—"

"We can," he said, and he pulled her into another hug. Then he held her at arm's length. "Let me look at you. You're getting thinner."

He looked different, too. His suit was rumpled, likely because he'd spent all day in a car, driving down here, but he looked older. Aged, with white hair at his temples and more wrinkles around his eyes. Still handsome, but also . . . not the man she knew, six months ago.

"I have some things to worry about," she said with a wink. "Kelsey?"

"She's with your parents while I'm attending my *conference*. It was too risky to bring her."

She nodded, then pulled herself away from him, as much as it hurt. She gathered up the rest of the things she'd left. "I know. I've got to go. And you should, too."

"Yeah."

She kissed him. "But I want you to know. I'm coming back to you. I promise. Tell Kelsey that I promise. I don't know how long it will take, but I'm working on it. Every day, I am. And I will never stop."

There were tears in his eyes, too. He gripped her shoulders hard, as if he refused to let her go. "You have to be careful. We miss you so much. And we know. We know you're doing everything you can. We are, too. Whatever you need . . ."

She couldn't ask that of them. Endangering them was the last thing she wanted to do. Even him being here was too risky. They needed to separate, at once. But doing so was like pulling her own heart from her body. She stifled a sob and pulled him close, savoring his touch, his smell.

"I love you," she whispered, and tore herself away from him. She couldn't stay longer. If she did, she was afraid she'd never want to let him go.

As she drove off, north on Route 90, she wiped the tears from her eyes. It had been amazing to see him, but also . . . not so good. Not only was it dangerous for him to do that, it reminded her of what she was missing out on, which made her heart ache worse than ever.

But it was what she needed. With people like Francine and Aiden believing in her, there was no way she wouldn't find the answers. She'd keep digging and digging until she did. The hitman might have been a dead end, but she couldn't stop thinking about the girl Kevin Reynolds had mentioned, before he died. There was a clue, there. And she wouldn't stop until she found the answers. She just needed to be careful and make the plan.

And one day, she would be able to come home to Kelsey and her husband . . . for good. She'd promised them that, and it was a promise she meant to keep, no matter what it took.

EPILOGUE

U.S. Marshal Kane Wilcox walked around the grounds of the Rising Sun commune, shaking his head. How the hell could anyone live like this?

The women were all dressed in rags, and they lived in hovels without any air conditioning. Wilcox had done several tours overseas while he was in the military, he'd lived in absolutely horrendous conditions, and yet, this was beyond the pale. Why anyone would choose this kind of lifestyle was unthinkable.

He walked over to the main building, the only nice structure on the grounds, where their leader must've lived. Guy looked like a real prick. Wilcox peeked in and confirmed it. Sure enough, he'd been living in the lap of luxury, letting his faithful "brothers" and "sisters" live like peasants. Really nice. Orwell had written books about stuff like this. Did this guy want his people to hate him?

"So, what's the deal?" he asked the nearest FBI agent as he finished filling up a squad car with residents of this fine establishment. "What's their crime?"

"Where do you want to start? Brent Brunley was wanted for some pretty hefty tax evasion," he said, counting on his fingers. "Paul Matthews is a wanted pedophile who skipped bail, Todd Bilson is wanted for domestic violence on his three previous wives . . ."

"Shit," Wilcox breathed. He'd known it was a hotbed of weirdness, but he'd had no idea how weird. So these people had all moved out here to avoid jail time. He scanned to the police car. They'd arrested a bunch of men, and a single woman, who was looking around in the back of the car, her eyes wild.

"And then there's the whole thing about forced polygamy that's been going on, here—"

"Polygamy. No kidding. So that's the Kool-Aid these people were drinking?" After everything he'd heard, nothing shocked him. "What's with the old lady?"

"Barbara Helvenson," he said, reading from his notepad. "She's the one who was weeding out the bad seeds among the recruits by offering them up to that psychopath who was arrested last night."

"Yeah . . . I read about that. So she pretended she was getting them to safety but what she was really trying to do was keep anyone from finding out the little jig they had going on here?"

"Yep. Seems that way. She was wanted for a string of crimes, passing bad checks, fraud, you name it, in LA," he shook his head. "A real piece of work. She found her little heaven here, and didn't want it to end, apparently."

"So . . . who's responsible?"

The officer looked up from his pad. "Huh?"

"You heard me. Who brought this whole thing down? Who cracked the case?"

The kid shrugged. "Got me. That's where it gets a little hazy. I think there was something about an anonymous call?"

Of course. A huge case like this, bringing in a number of wanted criminals, including a serial killer . . . and the person responsible for making it all happen preferred to remain anonymous?

He could smell the bullshit a mile away. He just needed to see if it was the brand of bullshit he was thinking of.

The Mia North brand. He'd found a little thread tying her to this area when he learned about Rachel Loring. And when it came to Mia North, he was beginning to realize that nothing was a coincidence. When there was smoke . . . she was usually nearby.

But he couldn't prove it. Not yet.

Wilcox nodded and headed into the air-conditioned office, where a couple of the girls from the commune were waiting. One was an older lady who was gnawing on her thumbnail. She was skinny as hell. "Hey," he said to her. "Can I get you something to eat?"

She shook her head. "I don't need food. I just saw that smug bastard Brent, arrested for everything he did. I'm content as can be!"

"So you didn't like him?" he asked, grabbing a pack of gum. He offered her the sleeve.

She took a piece and popped it into her mouth. "I didn't."

"But you didn't try to leave."

"No. 'Cause I knew that Barbie was fixing those girls. I had a feeling she was doing something, but I didn't know what. So I just stayed on and watched. And waited." She chewed noisily.

He fed a stick into his own mouth. “What’s your name?”

“Charlie.”

“Charlie,” he said, crossing his arms. “You seem like a pretty observant woman. You notice any new people, poking around, before this happened? Anything different?”

Charlie frowned. “Oh, a lot was different in the past few days.”

“Why’s that?”

“Because that’s when Sister Danielle came,” the woman said with a sly smile. “Second I saw her, I knew she would be different. She wouldn’t just stand there and take orders. I knew she was going to make trouble for them. And she did.”

He raised an eyebrow. “Where’s this Danielle, now? Can I talk to her?”

She shook her head. “Can’t. She’s gone. They say she died. I don’t believe it. I think she escaped. Without Barbie’s help, though. She was a smart one. Real nice, though. I liked her.”

He frowned. This was sounding all too familiar. “What did she look like?”

“Ah, hard to say. She had light brown hair. Long. Medium build. Pretty.”

“She’s gone?”

“Yeah . . . long gone.”

An officer nearby raised a finger. “But she did leave her belongings. They all did, supposedly, when they joined the commune.”

“Can I see it?”

The officer motioned him to a room, where he pulled out a canvas bag. He rifled through it, finding a bunch of clothes, a toothbrush, toothpaste. Nothing telling. “She didn’t have a phone?”

He shrugged. “Might’ve. If she did, someone removed it.”

He went through the stuff some more, pulling out a blue flannel shirt. He gritted his teeth. Mia North. No, none of this had her name on it, but he knew it. She’d been here. No, he didn’t have fingerprints or solid evidence. But he had that itch in the back of his head.

And why had she come here? Because she’d wanted to solve the mystery of what happened to her friend’s niece. That was a hell of a risk to take, but she’d done it. She’d solved the damn murder and put the guy behind bars, and she wasn’t even part of the force anymore.

He had to admit, that took some balls. He had to tip his hat to her. That was good work.

Didn't matter what good deeds she did, he told himself. Mia North could save the world from nuclear destruction. She was a wanted criminal, and his fugitive to find. And she was gone. Once again, he was a step behind. Like always.

But he was getting closer. No way would he give up, now.

"Thank you," he said, walking outside into the heat. He paced on the porch, the sweat soaking through his shirt, shaking his head. She'd been here. Right here. He was sure of it.

And though she might not have been here now, there was a little itch at the back of his head again, one that told him he was on the right track.

Just then, his phone rang with a call from Pembroke. It startled him, because service had been spotty ever since he'd driven out into the middle of this godforsaken no-man's-land.

"Hey," he said when Wilcox answered. "I heard you were down in Southwest Texas, and that you dropped everything and drove down there. What's that all about? You get a tip that Mia North is that far south?"

He took a deep breath and let it out. "No. It's unrelated. I'll be back in town, soon."

He ended the call so he wouldn't have to bullshit through any more questions. He might've been closer to Mia than he had been in days, but this little piece of information? He'd keep it to himself.

Right now, he wasn't sure what Mia was up to, but there were too many questions floating around that no one seemed to be able to answer.

But Mia could. He was sure of that. And this time, he'd get the answers directly from her.

NOW AVAILABLE!

<u>SEE HER VANISH</u>
(A Mia North FBI Suspense Thriller—Book 4)

When victims of a traveling "carnival killer" are found spread throughout the Southwest, the FBI is stumped, and fugitive FBI Agent Mia North must secretly help crack the case. But with Mia herself on the run, and being hunted by an elite U.S. Marshal, will she be able to catch this killer—and discover who framed her—before she herself is jailed?

"A brilliant book. I couldn't put it down and I never guessed who the murderer was!"
—Reader review for Only Murder

Special Agent Mia North is a rising star in the FBI—until, in an elaborate setup, she's framed for murder and sentenced to prison. When a lucky break allows her to escape, Mia finds herself a fugitive, on the run and on the wrong side of the law for the first time in her life. She can't see her young daughter—and she has no hope of returning to her former life.

The only way to get her life back, she realizes, is to hunt down whoever framed her.

But first, she must solve this case before the killer strikes again.

An action-packed page-turner, the MIA NORTH series is a riveting crime thriller, jammed with suspense, surprises, and twists and turns that you won't see coming. Fall in love with this brilliant new female protagonist and you'll be turning pages late into the night.

Books #5 and #6 in the series—SEE HER GONE and SEE HER DEAD—are now also available.

"I loved this thriller, read it in one sitting. Lots of twists and turns and I didn't guess the
culprit at all… Already pre-ordered the second!"
—Reader review for Only Murder

"This book takes off with a bang… An excellent read, and I'm looking forward to the next book!"
—Reader review for SEE HER RUN

"Fantastic book! It was hard to put down. I can't wait to see what happens next!"
—Reader review for SEE HER RUN

Rylie Dark

Debut author Rylie Dark is author of the SADIE PRICE FBI SUSPENSE THRILLER series, comprising six books (and counting); the MIA NORTH FBI SUSPENSE THRILLER series, comprising six books (and counting); the CARLY SEE FBI SUSPENSE THRILLER, comprising six books (and counting); and the MORGAN STARK FBI SUSPENSE THRILLER, comprising three books (and counting).

An avid reader and lifelong fan of the mystery and thriller genres, Rylie loves to hear from you, so please feel free to visit www.ryliedark.com to learn more and stay in touch.

BOOKS BY RYLIE DARK

SADIE PRICE FBI SUSPENSE THRILLER
ONLY MURDER (Book #1)
ONLY RAGE (Book #2)
ONLY HIS (Book #3)
ONLY ONCE (Book #4)
ONLY SPITE (Book #5)
ONLY MADNESS (Book #6)

MIA NORTH FBI SUSPENSE THRILLER
SEE HER RUN (Book #1)
SEE HER HIDE (Book #2)
SEE HER SCREAM (Book #3)
SEE HER VANISH (Book #4)
SEE HER GONE (Book #5)
SEE HER DEAD (Book #6)

CARLY SEE FBI SUSPENSE THRILLER
NO WAY OUT (Book #1)
NO WAY BACK (Book #2)
NO WAY HOME (Book #3)
NO WAY LEFT (Book #4)
NO WAY UP (Book #5)
NO WAY TO DIE (Book #6)

MORGAN STARK FBI SUSPENSE THRILLER
TOO LATE (Book #1)
TOO CLOSE (Book #2)
TOO FAR GONE (Book #3)

www.ingramcontent.com/pod-product-compliance
Lightning Source LLC
Chambersburg PA
CBHW030615310726
48979CB00003B/725

* 9 7 8 1 0 9 4 3 9 4 4 8 0 *